Lachlin MacTavish never had any trouble with the ladies, at least not until he caught the wandering eye of a pirate princess from the neighboring galaxy of Iwoehon. When she makes him an unwilling member of her intergalactic harem, female troubles take on a whole new meaning for Lachlin.

As blessings go, Emily Fairchild had more than her share of them back on Earth. Life was good for the blond-haired, blue-eyed beauty, but that all changed when she and her crewmates crashed on Tarilax. Surrounded by gorgeous masculine alien warriors, it sounded like heaven at first. But she can't even find one decent date. Regardless, she certainly didn't travel across the galaxy just to fall for a sexy, tattooed bad boy from Earth.

This book is a work of fiction. Names, characters, places, and incidents either are products of the author's imagination or are used fictitiously. Any resemblance to actual events or locales or persons, living or dead, is entirely coincidental.

His Sexy Duchess
Copyright © 2021 D. Morrissey
ISBN: 978-1-4874-3291-1
Cover art by Martine Jardin

Published by eXtasy Books Inc

Look for us online at:
www.eXtasybooks.com

His Sexy Duchess
Tarilean Adventures 3

By

D. Morrissey

PROLOGUE

Emily

Twelve years ago, when an energetic, well-polished recruiter from NASA stood in front of the entire sixth grade class at Carber Elementary and told us we could be whatever we wanted to be when we grew up, I believed him, dammit. And for the longest, it had seemed as though he'd been right.

Every educational award, academic achievement, and cum laude designation brought me one step closer to achieving my dreams. There had never been any question marks where my future was concerned. I was the golden child, the girl on fire, the woman with a plan. Life was simple and predictable, and best of all, easy. The good grades, the cushy jobs, the perfect boyfriends — all of it expected and taken for granted.

So when Commander Cora Carter told me that she and a few of her colleagues were going to save the Earth, rescue the ozone, and pioneer the next era of space exploration? Of course I freaking believed her. Why the hell wouldn't I?

The mission had sounded like a dream come true for someone like me, a Texas native with a double major in physics and aerospace engineering. According to Cora, it would be just like a road trip on Spring Break. Our five female crew would zip over to the edge of the galaxy, maybe shake a few alien hands, and bring back enough Marsonium to solve the world's energy and pollution problems for eons to come. Easy peasy, right? Eh, turns out, not so much.

So far, we've been attacked by Goridian pirates, sucked

1

into a black hole, and spit out on a planet where sabertooth butterflies and giant man-eating squirrels roam around in the wild preying on innocent humans. What sounded like an ideal mission, turned out to be a good dose of harsh old reality. My long-held belief system that hard work and honesty produced equitable results deserted me pretty quickly and was replaced with an irrevocable new truth, savage and cruel as it was. I would never have another triple, venti, half-sweet, non-fat, caramel macchiato again.

Lachlin

Okay, so maybe I've never been the perfect son, the perfect brother, or the perfect anything for that matter, but that didn't mean I wasn't crazy about the women in my life. My grandmother was a vision of statuesque beauty, my mother a living saint, and I swore there'd never been a more perfect girl created than my little sister, Aine. And what did these three women share in common that made them each special beyond compare? Me, that's what.

Growing up, I could seriously do no wrong. I was pampered and fussed over, spoiled and catered to, slathered with affection. To Nana and Mum, I was the sweetest, handsomest boy who had ever walked the Elm-lined streets of Arkansas. To my sister, Aine, I was the bravest, smartest protector any girl had ever had in the history of big brothers. In return, like my father, Bruce, I treasured and adored all three of the women in my life. Anywhere my dad left off, I stepped up, never failing to show them how much I loved them and I devoted I truly was.

When my nana and mum departed this world right on the heels of each other, the only person who took it harder than me was my dad. And the only thing that held us together was

Aine. Soft as silk, yet tough as nails when she had to be, my sister picked up mum's halo, adjusted it to her beautiful head, and carried on where they left off. That halo had fit her perfectly. Even though Dad and I often made things more difficult than they needed to be, she never once complained. And make no mistake, Dad and I were difficult. Where he'd fallen into a bottle of Irish whiskey for solace, I tumbled head-first into a new life of debauchery and loose women.

It was so easy. I'd always been a bit of a ladies' man, anyway. With my mum's pale Nordic beauty and my dad's strong Scottish features, I hit the genetics lottery. Too many women seemed prone to swooning and throwing themselves at my feet for it not to be true. Hell, I didn't even have to try. I knew I looked good. And if my Dad was anything to go by, I'd probably just look better with age. My first sexual encounter was with a babysitter, and I learned soon enough that most women were eager, nay anxious, to fall beneath my particular sword of seduction. But, even so, I adored each and every one of them.

In fact, I was on my way home one night after having adored one of these women for several hours when I learned that even alien females weren't immune to my special kind of charm. Aliyah Azandar, daughter of Kwanlo Azandar, Emperor of the Iwoehan system snatched me from a field behind my favorite pub and added me to her harem as a royal concubine. After our first mating, Aliyah named me chief consort and declared me property of the crown. Until I wasn't.

CHAPTER ONE

Emily

"I am not freaking wearing that."

Cora has obviously lost her mind. I can't believe she'd even have the nerve to ask. Why, I've got bandanas that would cover more skin than that dress.

"It's just one night, Em. One tiny dinner," Cora whines and makes little goo-goo eyes at me. "It would make Fina and the boys so happy."

Crossing my arms over my chest, I purse my lips and shake my head. "Do not use the babies to try and guilt me, Cora. They're barely old enough to walk. They wouldn't care if Aunt Emmy showed up naked."

"Well, they might not care, but I bet Counselor Ja'Baal would love it." Cora laughs as she makes one more broad sweep across my lashes with the mascara brush.

Maggie nods. "Yeah, and if he doesn't, you can always count on Counselor Irston."

"Ew!"

All five of us gag at the thought of dining naked with Irston.

If Fred Flintstone and Marge Simpson had had a love child, it would look like Counselor Irston. Even so, it's not his looks that make him so unattractive. The man is evil from the tip of his pitchfork right down to the very soles of his cloven hooves. And much to the chagrin of Tarilax, his daughter, Minova, is a chip off the old block.

4

"I agree with Emily," Shauna states in her Siri voice. Her normally blank face is puckered with distaste, which is our only hint that she's speaking with emotion. "You shouldn't be using her this way, Cora. Women have struggled too long and worked too hard to be objectified for the amusement of men."

"Mackis," Cora corrects. "The Tarileans call men *mackis*."

Maggie unwinds the curling iron from my hair and shakes it at Shauna. "Girl, get a grip. This isn't the twentieth century anymore, and in case you've forgotten, we aren't exactly on Earth anymore, either. If anyone gets objectified here on Tarilax, it's the *mackis*, not the women."

"Femkis," Cora interjects, offering the Tarilean term for women.

"You ain't lying, sister. These *femkis* are brutal, and they have the goods to back it up. I haven't seen one yet that didn't make me look like a petite flower."

Lisa, our chief security officer whom we refer to affectionately as the Arkansas Amazon, is sitting at the small desk in my room, her feet propped casually on top of the blueprint mock-ups for my new deluxe starship cruiser that will eventually carry my sad ass back to Earth. I hope.

"There. I'm done." Cora sits back in her chair to examine her handiwork.

"Me, too," Maggie says as she takes special care fluffing a banana-sized curl draped across my shoulder. "Just let me—" She doesn't bother finishing the sentence. She just spritzes me one more time with the liquid glue she insists on calling hairspray.

"Perfect!" Cora gestures toward the mirror, my cue to ooh and aah and pronounce them both makeover geniuses responsible for changing the course of my fucked up life.

"Mm hm. Fine. Now, what am I supposed to wear?"

I stare at myself in the mirror. Honestly, I can't believe it's me. Cora did an incredible job. My smoky eyes linger on my curled lashes and blushed cheeks, coming to rest finally on a pair of highly glossed, neglected lips that haven't seen any snogging action for far too long. I finger my delicately teased hair, wondering how it can look so effortlessly messy after Maggie spent so much time on it. Still, it looks great, and I love it, all of it. Of course, I'd never let them know that.

"What do you mean, *fine*? Just fine?" Maggie places her hands on her hips, narrowing her eyes at me in the mirror.

"Honey, you look hot! Like freaking model hot. *Fine* doesn't even begin to cover it." Cora smiles at my reflection. "All you need is this dress."

She shakes the skimpy garment at me.

I sigh and close my eyes, not quite ready to admit defeat. "Look, if this Counselor Ja'Baal is so damn important, let Maggie seduce him. She's got a hell of a lot more experience at that than I do."

"Hey, hey," Maggie makes a half-hearted attempt to appear offended. "First of all, I'm not sure that was a compliment. Secondly, I am sure Nordric wouldn't be very happy if I started flirting with Ja'Baal. And lastly, it's not me that Ja'Baal is infatuated with, my friend. It's you."

"Maggie's right, Em." Cora gets up and carefully spreads the dress on my bed. "You know I wouldn't ask you to do this if it wasn't important to Horok. Heck, to all of us. Ja'Baal is the newest member of the Intergalactic Committee of Science and Technology. He has the power to push our agenda to the other ICST members. Em, this may be our best chance to reconnect with Earth."

"Fine. I'll wear the stupid dress." I cave. I always cave. "But only for Fina and the boys."

Actually, there's not much I wouldn't do for Cora's and Horok's one-year-old triplets. Half Tarilean, they're big for their age, but they're precious little gems. Maybe it's because I'm biased, but they're the most beautiful babies ever produced. The only exception I might be able to concede is Aine and Griz's baby, Theo, who just so happens to be half Tarilean, too. We'd all do anything in our power to give those babies a chance to know the human side of their heritage, and not just the Tarilean.

Cora hops up and down, clapping her hands like baby Fina, as if she doesn't always get her way.

"Do you realize how much you've changed since you had the babies, Commander?"

She grins as though I've just given her a compliment. "Totally worth it. You'll see someday."

"Yeah, I doubt it." Maybe once upon a time, I would have believed that, but my life turned into a shit storm the day we were shot out of the sky by Goridian pirates, and it has only gotten worse since then. How many people can get dropped onto a planet with a billion gorgeous, musclebound god-like warriors and not be able to find even one serious contender for a boyfriend? Well, I can tell you, from our original crew, only one. Me.

When I pick up the dress, my stomach clenches as the magnitude of what I've just agreed to sinks in.

"Why does it have to be at the freaking Moon Bistro? There's two square miles of gorgeous castle here with more dining rooms than I can count. Yet, we have to take a space shuttle to get to a restaurant? Who all is going to this fancy-schmancy dinner party, anyway?"

Cora shrugs. "Apparently, it's only a short fifteen minute flight to the Fisan Moon, and the view of Tarilax from the Moon Bistro is supposed to be spectacular. As far as I know, it'll just be us, Horok's mom and dad, and a few of the councilors and their wives. You know, an intimate dinner party hosted by Irston to celebrate Ja'Baal's appointment to the ICST. It's mostly couples, which is why Irston was pretty insistent that Horok bring you along. I think we all know why."

Cora gives me an evil grin.

Shauna yawns. "You know, I'm surprised Irston is even going along with Ja'Baal's interest in Emily. I would think he'd be pushing Minova on Ja'Baal the way he did with Horok."

"Don't make me gag," Maggie snips, poking a well-manicured finger in and out of her mouth.

I swear Cora growls. "Yeah. Sometimes, I think she still hasn't gotten the message that Horok is off the market. But, you're right. He'd be pushing Minova on Ja'Baal in a heartbeat if he didn't have his sights already set on Horok's brother."

Interesting. Horok has several brothers. They're all nice-looking, but they feel like family, and they're all younger than he is. "Which one?"

"Vexel."

"Uh . . . The one who's still in high school?"

What the hell? Aren't there laws here that protect kids from that sort of thing?

"Yep." Cora's eyes get wide, and she shakes her head. "Vexel will be of legal age next month, even though he doesn't graduate until later this year. I'm telling you, Irston doesn't really care who he marries Minova off to so long as it's a member of the royal family with an uncontested tie to the crown."

"What a jerk," Shauna remarks. "Cora, you may want to keep a close eye on the babies. He may decide Jordy and Griffin are next in line for Minova."

"Over my dead body! I swear, I don't think his wife really died on that warship. I think she threw herself in front of a photon torpedo just to get away from Irston's sick ass."

Wow. That was harsh, even for Lisa.

"Come on. Let's give Emily some privacy so she can finish getting dressed." Lisa stands and stretches, the alien fabric of her new security uniform molding to her curves like a second skin. "I need to make sure our taxi has arrived, anyway. Who all's riding with Eff and Lachlin?"

"Just Emily, Maggie and Shauna. Oh, and you, of course," Cora replies with a wink. She always winks when she mentions Lisa and Eff in a sentence together. I swear it's like she's in junior high again.

"What about Aine and Griz? And Bruce and Li'andra? Don't they want to ride with Lachlin?"

Since Aine and her father, Bruce, have been rescued from slavers a few months ago, they've reunited with Aine's brother, Lachlin, and the three of them have been damn near inseparable. But really, who can blame them? I've heard that Lachlin was abducted even before Aine and Bruce were. I don't know all the details, but Horok said that he caught the eye of some evil empress who took him and used him as her own personal boy toy. I've only gotten a quick glimpse of the man, but from what I saw, I can understand why. The guy is freaking gorgeous.

"They're riding with us," Cora says. "Since Aine is mated to Griz, Horok's cousin, and Bruce is dating Griz's mother, the queen's sister, they're stuck with us. I'm sure they'd rather be riding with Lachlin, though."

"So you'll be on Air Force One with the king and the rest of the royal party," Lisa smirks.

Cora giggles. "The Tariroyal Cruiser, yes."

"All right, then. Everyone riding with Eff and Lachlin, be at the south entrance by seven. Got it?"

Everyone nods and disperses, leaving me alone to frown at my dress. I now know how a sacrificial virgin feels right before the volcano swallows her up. Not that I believe Councilor Ja'Baal should be compared to a fiery death, and not because I'm a virgin, either, because I'm not. I just don't like the idea of parading around in front of Ja'Baal looking like a nerdy hooker, leading him on as if he had a chance in hell of getting anywhere with me. He doesn't, which is too bad really because unlike Irston, he seems like a decent guy. There's just no chemistry there. You know, my body isn't burning with intense desire, my loins haven't suddenly burst into flame, that sort of thing.

I sigh and start stripping. Oh, well. What's the worst that can happen?

Chapter Two

Lachlin

"You sure you don't want me to drive so you and Lisa can have a few minutes of alone time?" I smirk and waggle my brows at Eff.

The poor guy can't seem to catch a break where that girl's concerned. It's like the universe is one big cosmic cockblocking nightmare.

"No."

"Shall I send her to the bridge to deliver a 'special' message to you?"

"No."

I've only been an engineer on Epherus' crew aboard the Wraith for a short time, but I should be getting used to his sullen moody ass by now. I mean, I'm no big talker by any means, but even I could stand more than three words over a three-day period. Already, his strange blue color has stopped shocking me every time I see him, and his horns don't freak me out as much as they did at first. I've even adjusted to the long sharp quills that pop out of his forearms when he's pissed, but I cannot go a whole week without talking.

"Whatever." I shrug. "Just trying to do you a solid, man."

"I am not a *man*," he growls.

Oops. He's right. He's male, for sure. Just not technically a man. Epherus Zinto—Eff to his friends if he can truly claim any—is from some planet called Aurelia IV. It's kind of a weird name since as far as I know, there's no I, II or III. There are, however, a lot of giant blue guys on IV with horns and pointy spines walking around growling and kicking the shit out of each other. Obviously, they're an aggressive species with a high demographic of assassins and mercenaries.

"My bad," I sigh while I strap in.

I watch him closely as he steers the ship into the landing bay at the spaceport on Tarilax's royal admin grounds. So far, I think Tarilax is the most beautiful planet I've seen on my unplanned tour of the universe. It's like a version of Earth from a million years ago, prehistoric and pristine. Or, at least, what it looked like before we lost the seasons, before Earth's ozone crapped out.

The Wraith comes to rest in a perfect landing right in front of the spaceport marshalers, who give us a nod and immediately move on to the next vessel requesting entrance. There seems to be a lot of them, too.

"What's going on? I've never seen this place so busy before."

"The rotational Festival of Lights is tomorrow," Eff says, powering down the ship and flipping off his harness. "They're celebrating Ophelia, the Goddess of Love and Light."

I follow suit, unbuckling my harness and falling in behind him to disembark. "Well, that's interesting. So, they believe in this love goddess. Do you—"

"No."

I chuckle as we step off the ship and merge into the diverse crowd gathered along the tarmac. I'd like to know more about tomorrow's festival, but I won't get anything else out of Eff right now. He's too busy scouring the crowd for any enemies who might want to kill him—you know, Pelophesian assassins, Ranin mercs, Iwoehon pirates, disgruntled ex-girlfriends. That sort of thing. I don't really expect any trouble, though. The guy's just totally paranoid, which probably has something to do with his being a ruthless contract killer.

"Lachlin! Epherus!"

Damn. After all that time apart, I can't get used to the sight of my little sister again. Every single time I spot her, I lose my fucking breath. In the year I was away, she changed. Really changed. She grew up, and looks so much like our mum, it's almost eerie. Standing there beside our pop, Bruce, she makes my heart clench.

I toss my chin, letting her know that I see her, then start elbowing my way through the crowd toward her and Bruce. They meet me halfway, Aine pulling me into a bear hug and squealing like I didn't just see her last week. It's fine, though. She still hasn't gotten over me disappearing on her for a year. Not sure she ever will. Not sure I ever will, either.

"Hey, bro! Hey, Eff!" Aine beams at me and the moody bastard beside me, her hands gripping my arms like I might try to run away.

"Aine. Bruce. Griz."

Eff nods and greets each one of them, which is a really friendly greeting for an Aurelian, from what I'm told. I know he thinks a lot of Bruce and Griz, Aine's husband.

"You sure look nice, sis." I mean it, too. Fancy new dress and all dolled up, she could win a beauty contest. I love seeing her this way, happiness wafting off her like expensive perfume. "You even got the old man cleaned up."

"Watch it, lad." Bruce wrenches me away from Aine, clasping my forearm firmly while he pounds on my back. His eyes sparkle with pride as he examines me, and fuck if I don't almost choke up. "Good to see you, Lach."

"You, too, Pop."

"Let's get out of the way," Griz says, guiding Aine toward a quiet spot near one of the spaceport cafes.

I follow along, glad for the chance to walk off this sudden case of sentiment. Time to lighten the mood. "Are you guys riding with us, Ainie?"

"No, we're going with Cora and Horok," she says sadly. "Not that I mind," she adds hastily, cutting her eyes to Griz.

"Sorry, sweetling. I didn't get a say in the travel arrangements this time," Griz replies.

"It's fine, guys. Don't worry about it. You can ride with me next time."

I reach out my hand to pat Aine on the head and quickly catch myself. It looks like someone's spent hours fixing her hair, and I'm sure she wouldn't be too happy if I mussed it. I keep forgetting she's not a little kid anymore. Hell, she has a kid now, not to mention a huge, badass Tarilean warrior for a husband who'd probably kick my ass if I upset her. Speaking of my nephew, I was hoping to see him. "Where's Theo?"

"He's with Horok's mate," Griz replies. "He'll be staying in the royal nursery with the triplets tonight."

Well, la de fucking da. Of course he will be. Frowning, I shake my head. Royal this, and royal that. Aine's in-laws are turning into a royal pain in the ass. I was hoping to get to hold the little fella tonight. It may not be considered macho or manly, but I love kids, even babies. And Aine's may be the closest I ever get to having one of my own.

"I'm sorry, Lach. Come over tomorrow, and you can play with him as long as you want." Aine gives me a bright smile, her eyes wide and hopeful.

"Gee, I would, but not sure what we're doing tomorrow." I arch my brows at Eff to see if he might give any clues. It's not like we keep regular office hours. We go where the work is, wherever there's someone or something that needs killing.

"We're coming in for the light festival," he says, totally blowing my mind.

My jaw falls open. "Pardon?"

"What?" he snaps.

"I don't think I heard you correctly. Did you say we're

coming back here to see Lisa?"

He growls and narrows his eyes.

"Ooh . . . We're coming back for the *festival*." I smile like a jackass. I'm really just yanking his dick. I like to watch his eyes get all squinty and killer-y when I tease him.

Aine and Griz snigger, enjoying themselves at Eff's expense.

"Aye! That's braw!" Bruce chimes in, clueless as usual. "Griz will get us some more of that kocho whisky, which is a fine sight better than all that fizzy juice Li'andra's been serving me up. Aine can scruff us up some haggis and a toffee pudding. That's well tidy scran right there."

"I can do that," Aine replies, smiling joyously. "Except I'll have to improvise a bit on your haggis. I don't exactly have a herd of yummy sheep running around in my backyard, but I suppose we can try some of those skeeps instead. Maybe I'll invite the girls, too. Would you like to join us, Eff?"

I bite my lip and try not to smile. Everyone knows that Eff is in love with Lisa. Everyone except Eff, that is. Lisa is a total badass, too. A hot badass who's also from Arkansas, just like me and Aine. She's tall and stacked, with short wavy hair and a pretty face. I can totally see the appeal, if you're into chicks like that, meaning ones who can kick your ass when they get mad at you.

Eff grunts, dipping his chin briefly. For an emotionally constipated Aurelian, that's the same as saying, 'Why, fuck yeah. I'd love to come. Thank you so much for inviting me'.

I think Aine knows this, too. She gives Eff her brilliant megawatt smile as she clutches Griz's arm excitedly. I gotta say, I didn't care much at first for the pretty Tarilean playboy who knocked up my sister. I mean, it's a huge deal entrusting your baby sister to another jackass like me with Peter Pan Syndrome. But, so far, the way he treats her and Bruce, I got no issues with the guy. He's all right in my book.

"Aine!"

We turn around to see Horok with a six-pack of hot chicks waving at us from across the marketplace. My eyes roll past each of them until they settle on one in particular, one that now has my dick's full attention. Who the hell is that?

A breathtaking beauty with the sweet face of an angel and big blue eyes that would guarantee a free pass to commit murder. Her long blond hair is thick and curly, the ends resting nicely on top of a pair of exquisite tits. It's those legs, though. Those legs are the fucking crème de la crème of stems. They're long and lean and on full display in that short little dress she's wearing.

Yeah, she's a knockout, all right, but a little too innocent for me. I get the feeling she's not into Scottish bad boys with tattoo sleeves and a shit-ton of crazy, anyway. She stands a little apart from the other girls, her back stiff and her shoulders square. Her chin tilts toward the ceiling like she's looking down her nose at all the people passing by. That settles it. Rich, entitled girls are just not my cup of java, and this one acts like she's the fucking Duchess of York.

"Cora! Guys! Over here!" Aine shouts at the flock of females.

Eff stiffens beside me as the group makes their way over to the café, and all of a sudden, I hear this weird choking noise that I swear is coming from him. That's when I notice Lisa, walking beside the duchess with her eyes locked on Eff. I've never seen a scarier, more murder-y dude than Eff, and to watch him turn into a wobbly puddle of jelly by a chick is fucking hilarious. In fact, I would be busting a nut laughing right now if I hadn't glanced up and found the duchess' eyes locked on me.

Faintly, I hear that choking noise again, quickly realizing it's coming from me this time. Holy fucking cow. Those eyes. Those big, round eyes of hers could make an honest man turn on his brother, so honest and pure. They hide nothing. Or maybe they hide everything?

While the others bounce around hugging each other, jabbering away like long-lost cousins, Lisa strolls straight up to where Eff and I are standing, never taking her eyes off him, and grins right into his scowling blue face.

"Eff," she says, pretty as you please. Damn. This girl has a mean streak a mile wide.

Poor Eff doesn't say a word, his face totally blank, and I can't tell if it's his normal blank face, or if he's just too damn petrified to speak. Thank fuck he's stopped making that whimpering noise.

"Lachlin!"

I peel my eyes away from the lovelorn couple in front of me long enough to answer my sister. "Yeah?"

"I can't remember who all you've met." She starts clicking off a roster full of names that I'm never going to remember, even though I've met them all before, I think, except for the very last one. "And, this is Emily."

"Hello, Lachlin."

Okay. Now, I am well and truly fucked. Face like an angel, voice as sweet as honey, and my name on her lips makes me hard as steel.

"Duchess." I nod, unable to do anything about my shit-eating grin.

Her finely plucked brows draw together, and she tilts her head the tiniest bit.

That's right, sweetheart. I said 'duchess.'

Aine's knowing smile confirms she's onto me before Cora's husband interrupts.

"There's my sire." Horok waves across the way to a procession of vehicles that looks like floating golf carts headed for the launch bays. "We should go."

After several long drawn-out farewells, which is ridiculous since most of them are all going to the same place, half the group splinters off. Those left behind are riding with me and Eff.

"Everyone ready?" I have to force myself to stop eye-fucking the duchess long enough to feign interest in Aine's other friends.

After a few head nods and random yeps, we turn to make our way back to Eff's ship. When we get there, I notice several other passengers lingering around the entrance, and it becomes abundantly clear that I need to pull my head out of my ass. I totally forgot about the extra fares we booked for Fison. Still being somewhat new to Eff's crew, I can't afford these kinds of slip-ups.

"An intimate dinner, my ass," Duchess grumbles beneath her breath as she takes in the crowd.

Apparently, she's surprised by the number of guests, but I'm not. These types always go overboard on their hoity-toity soirées. Most of the extra fares are important enough to get invited, but not high-ranking enough to ride in the royal cruiser. Doesn't matter to me. It's extra money in my pocket. I set to work immediately lowering the boarding gear, stowing bags, and herding the group into some semblance of an organized line.

We're down to just me and Eff and Aine's friends, and my hand is getting twitchy because I intend to place it on the duchess' ass when I personally escort her inside. It's been a long time since I was interested in a girl, really interested, but I think she might just be worth the time and effort.

Unfortunately, my plan turns to shit before I have a chance to implement. We don't even make it onto the boarding ramp before the first crisis hits.

Chapter Three

Lisa

The station is a madhouse today. No surprise. I knew it would be crazy with the Council dinner tonight and the Festival of Lights kicking off tomorrow. The spaceport is jam-packed with decorations for the celebration, and it reminds me a lot of Christmas back home.

Bright-colored streamers wriggle around the ceiling like long rainbow snakes, and strings of red and blue lights hang from beams along the walkway. Everywhere I look, tiny tokens of Ophelia the Goddess of Light and Love, sit perched on shelves and tabletops, bric-a-brac filling every little nook and cranny.

"I'm so sorry! Light blessings be upon you," a tall, red woman with silver hair says as she bumps into us, her arms full of packages.

I have to do a double-take. The woman is taller than I am, and I'm over six feet. Even that is easily overlooked, though, by the fact that she's red. I don't just mean sunburned kind of red. I mean lobster kind of red, firetruck red. And while she doesn't seem to have any pincers, she does have three tits. Three! Big ones, too, with pert, poky nipples and cleavage that leaves no room for imagination. Don't even get me started on her silver hair. Thick strands of tinsel that shoot out from her scalp every which way.

"Oh, no worries," Emily replies with a bright smile as she bows at the woman. "And may love light your way, as well."

We learned yesterday that's the appropriate response to the light blessings greeting. People have been spewing it at us all week. I've just been nodding back with a slack look on my face.

"Have a happy festival," the woman says as she sashays away.

We stare at her back until she's no longer in sight, then look at each other and shrug.

"What species was that?" Shauna asks, still frowning at the corner where the woman disappeared.

"I don't know for sure. Triboobians?" I giggle.

"Breastgalorians?" Maggie chuckles.

"No, no. Tripletittians," I suggest, laughing so hard now, my eyes water.

We stand there giggling like a bunch of school girls for a few minutes. Never in my life would I have suspected that so many different species and races coexisted in this vast universe. And just like back home, if you want to see all of them, just hang out at a central travel hub for a while. The spaceport is full of them. Tall ones, short ones, plump ones, flat ones, every color under the sun. Some have two hands, some have four. I've even seen beings with several sets of lips and jelly-looking bodies, and things that look like carpets with limbs. And now, three-breasted ones!

"Come on," I tell them, flapping my arms like a mother hen. "We need to find our gate."

We start inching our way forward again, gawking at all the shops and vendors. It looks like hundreds of merchants have set up tents and lean-tos all along the breezeways, hawking their wares from both sides of the aisle.

"Hey! You there!" I turn my head to see a man — and I use that term loosely — who looks like a centipede with a hairpiece pointing a walking stick at me. "Yes, you. I'm talking to you."

I shake my head at him and cut my eyes toward Shauna. I

nod at her and smile as if we're having an engaging conversation, one that he shouldn't dream of interrupting. She arches her brow at me like I'm nuts.

"Come over here, pretty female, and let me show you this new travel groomer I just got in. It has seventy-five different settings that can handle anything from full-body hair to eyebrows alone. It includes toothbrushes for up to five mouths and holds a whole gallon of mouthwash at one time. All this and the entire device can fit right into your pocket. You'll never want to go anywhere else without it again. I guarantee it."

I roll my eyes at Shauna.

"Well, he guarantees it." She giggles.

I sigh and shake my head, trying to elbow a path for us through the unwieldy mob of holiday trekkers. I'll never understand why they insist on jamming their cities so full of people when there's like a trillion acres of wild, untamed jungle out there that could be easily developed for use. But, no. We're all crammed in here like sardines in a tin can.

People are flitting around everywhere, bumping and jostling us, blessing us, and blocking traffic with all the bowing and greeting going on. It's all I can do to keep our little group together when I hear a deep voice beckon from behind us.

"Oh! There's Horok and Cora!" Maggie says, pushing us over to the edge so they can catch up.

"Geez! I can't believe we found you in this nuthouse," Cora says when they finally reach us. "We'll never find the rest of our group in here."

Immediately, Shauna starts jumping up and down and pointing.

"Look! There they are! Aine!" she calls out, waving like a crazy woman over the top of the crowd. I guess she fits right in with the rest of the mob.

I turn around, my eyes roving past all the different faces

and species until I finally see what I'm looking for. My heart skitters to a halt, then makes up for lost time by beating out a Meringue in my chest. I feel lightheaded, my knees weak and wobbly. Sweat breaks out across my forehead, beneath my boobs and lower back. Shit, I'm having a panic attack.

"Oh, Lisa! There's Eff." Cora laughs.

"Isn't that Lachlin with him?" Emily asks, the interest in her voice clear even though she's trying hard to disguise it.

I stand there for a moment, taking deep breaths as I look into the dark, penetrating eyes of the indigo-colored male across the platform. Tall and broad-shouldered, he stands out from the crowd, even the Tarileans who are practically giants compared to us.

Epherus Zinto has got to be the sexiest man in the entire freaking universe.

Cora places her hand into my back and pushes me forward into the pedestrian traffic. I keep my eyes on the blue Adonis across the way until the next distraction sucks me in.

"Omega spray?" a vendor shouts as he squirts a bottle of scent into the crowd around us. "Need to catch that certain Alpha in your life who always seems to get away? One small squirt of Omega spray, and your Alpha won't be able to resist you. Come and get this powerful love potion created by the witches of Salemni and blessed by the Goddess of Light and Love herself. You'll be glad you did. I guarantee it."

For a second, I'm actually tempted to stop and buy a few gallons, then the moment passes, and I continue shuffling forward in the direction of our friends. I can do this. I know I can. I will bag my blue Alpha, without the help of some stupid love potion. I will show no fear. I will take no prisoners. I will triumph, and I will get laid!

I'm still repeating these encouraging words to myself when we get there. They must be working, too, because I march straight up to the gorgeous blue beefcake and smile right into his handsome face.

"Eff," I purr.

He says nothing, just keeps staring at me with a blank look on his face. I stare back for at least a full minute, smiling like a jackass while my confidence bleeds out onto the floor and wishing a meteor or a small house would crash through the ceiling and land on top of me. Fortunately, I'm saved by my coms unit as it signals an incoming call.

"Excuse me," I murmur as though I'm disengaging from an actual conversation.

I hustle over to an empty corner by the nearby café and raise my wrist in front of me. The little black device on my wrist flashes red and beeps until I speak into it.

"Respond coms," I tell it.

Immediately, Nanny Orenda's miniature image appears before me.

"Greetings, Lisa," she says, her soft maternal voice full of its usual warmth and kindness.

"Nanny Orenda! Hello. Is everything okay?"

"I'm afraid not," she says, shaking her head. "The babysitter has not yet arrived, and it's past time for me to go to the Light Chapel."

"I see. Did you try calling her?"

"Yes, I did. Several times, in fact. She didn't answer. That's why I'm calling you. It's not just because I need to get to the chapel, even though I do. I'm directing the children's play this year, you know."

I nod and purse my lips impatiently. She's only waxed on about this stupid play for the last month. "Yes, Nanny, I know."

"I'm just worried about Cyntina. It's not like her to be late or to ignore a call from the royal house. I'm afraid there's something wrong. Something bad has happened."

"It's probably just the holiday traffic," I tell her as I glance up at the zoo around me. "You wouldn't believe all the people here at the station."

"You're probably right," she says wistfully. "I guess those males from Aurelia just scared me a little. I'm feeling a bit out of sorts."

"What males from Aurelia?" The only Aurelian male I know on Tarilax is Eff.

"Oh, I ran into a couple of them downstairs in the foyer earlier. I wouldn't have thought much about it, but they were acting suspicious. I think one of them actually had a weapon beneath his tunic. Right there in the administration offices!"

Shit. That's not good. I'll have to ask Eff if he has any friends in the area.

"Okay. Well, did you ask them why they were there?"

"No, but I heard one of them say that someone, a female, was supposed to meet them downstairs. I just hope it wasn't Cyntina."

I sigh, chewing on my lip as I try to decide what to do. This could be nothing. Or, it could be really bad.

"Okay, Nanny. Just stay there and hang tight. I'll send someone back to take over for you."

She smiles with relief. "Oh, thank you, Lisa. I knew I could count on you."

I nod and disconnect the call. Well, hell. I can't go back. I'm supposed to coordinate protection for Horok and Cora tonight. If I don't show up, there will be a huge gap in their security.

Eff and the others are nowhere in sight as I meander back to the spot where I left them. We don't have time for this. I stand on my tiptoes and crane my head in every direction, searching for a big blue alien standing around with a horde of little humans.

"My dam! Look at that one!"

I glance down to see a small child with the face of a pug

pointing up at me and giggling. Giggling. At me.

"It's so . . . plain and ugly."

"Shh. Peaches!" its mother with a face like a Pekinese scolds. "That's very rude. We never talk about others that way when they can hear us. They can't help the way they were born."

Is she kidding me? With a face like that? And don't get me started on her parenting skills. *Pfft.*

"I'm so sorry," she says to me, a sympathetic look on her face. "Kids. I suppose they have to learn."

"Uh . . . sure." I turn around and make my way through the throng of holiday travelers, heading toward the departure gates.

Maybe that's why Eff hasn't asked me out? Does he think I'm plain and ugly, too? Maybe he prefers women with canine faces? And manners like a pig, I chuckle. I know it takes all kinds. There must be males out here who prefer Pekinese women if there are children running around who look like pugs.

I suppose I can see how I'd look plain and ugly to them. I mean, I don't have a black button nose or long wispy whiskers that stick out from beneath it. I don't have perky ears on top of my head or big round eyes the size of dinner plates. And I sure don't have fur covering my entire face, or a tail nubbin poking out from the back of my pants. Damn. I am plain.

Finally, I see my friends. Shauna and Maggie are watching as several people make their way up the boarding plank onto Eff's ship while he stands there casually talking to Lachlin. It looks like they've already started boarding. Without me!

"Hey!" I call out, but they ignore me. I start running in case they finish boarding and decide to actually leave without me. "Wait!"

CHAPTER FOUR

Emily

He called me Duchess. Lachlin MacTavish, hot, sexy inter-galactic sex god, called me Duchess. Lachlin. MacTavish. I have no idea why he called me that, but now, my palms are sweaty, my heart is racing, and everything I say sounds all breathy and desperate.

Oh, God. Please tell me I am not *that* girl. The one who titters and swoons like a simpleton whenever a hot, hunky bad boy shows her the slightest bit of attention. No way am I that girl. I am an intelligent, level-headed woman who appreciates a nice, well-mannered gentleman with morals and a 401-K, not tattoos and 401 condoms in his wallet. He is so not my type. So why do I keep trying to think of ways to get him to touch me?

"Wait!" Lisa calls as she jogs across the tarmac. She marches straight over to Lachlin and Eff, panting and shaking her head. Maggie, Shauna and I edge closer so we can eavesdrop on the conversation. "We have a problem."

Eff steps closer to her as he eyes her up and down, his horns perking up, and the quills on his arms starting to quiver. "What is it? What's wrong?"

A shudder rolls through me. I don't get what she sees in that guy. He hardly ever speaks, he looks angry all the time, he's blue, and he has freaking horns, for Pete's sake. I'm not even going to mention those sharp pointy spines on his arms.

"I just got a call from Nanny Orenda," Lisa says. "The

babysitter hasn't shown up yet, and they can't reach her by com."

"Have Cora and Aine taken off yet?" Shauna stands on her tiptoes and tries to peer over the top of the crowd.

"Yes."

See what I mean? That's all Eff says. Freaking 'yes'. How helpful is that?

"Well, who's staying here with the babies, then?" Lisa looks at each of us.

"Me! I will." I throw my hand in the air so fast, I nearly slap Lachlin. That would be just my luck these days, too. I swear the universe is out to get me.

"Uh . . . Good try, but no. You have to go." Maggie smirks.

Well, crap. I tried. Glancing down at my flimsy cocktail dress, I want to choke Cora all over again. That's when I notice Lachlin from the corner of my eye, checking out my flimsy cocktail dress, too. He's probably wondering why I *have* to go.

Dammit. Quit staring at me. Now I'm nervous, and I can't decide what expression I should be wearing. Should I smile? Smirk? Scowl? Anything that starts with an S? I try to relax my features, but it feels like every single muscle in my face is twitching. He's going to think I have some kind of facial tic disorder.

"Well, I can't stay," Lisa muses.

"Don't look at me. Nordric's waiting for me there. We haven't been together in weeks, and I'm not missing it." Maggie shakes her head for emphasis.

We all turn to look at Shauna, who fidgets with her glasses. "Don't look at me, either. We're unveiling the new immunization formula for space influenza tonight right after dinner. It's finally been formally approved by the UFDA, and the Council has been keeping it under lock and key."

"That's because their intelligence agency learned of several plots to steal it," Maggie says. "There's a lot of money and power at stake, not to mention lives if it were to fall into the hands of some nefarious element or corrupt government. Can you imagine what would happen if the Lizentines got ahold of it?"

"I know. Just seemed a little paranoid to me. Still, Horok will kill me if I don't show up."

Slowly, they all turn to look at me again, and I giggle. Actually, it's more like an evil laugh. This might be my lucky day, after all.

"Well, hell." Lisa frowns.

"Just go." I wave my hand like it's no big deal. "I'll stay here until the babysitter shows, and then, I'll grab a shuttle and meet you guys there." I really have no intention of going.

"By yourself? I don't think so." The look on Lisa's face brooks no argument.

"I'll stay with her."

My head whips around, and I find Lachlin still gazing at me, a lazy grin on his stupid, handsome face.

"Uh . . ." I'm not sure that's a good idea.

Let me lay my cards on the table here. I haven't had sex in over a year, and I'm simply not strong enough at the moment to resist Lachlin MacTavish, the Scottish super stud who gobbles up little virgins for breakfast. Plus, he won't stop staring at me.

The Emily-Fairchild-hotness-meter currently rates him at a threat level red, which means imminent risk of legs falling open. The man has my hormones popping like kettle corn, and for whatever reason, my brain shuts off whenever he looks at me, which seems to be all the freaking time.

"Com me every sixty clicks on the nines to check in," Eff says to Lach before turning his steely gaze back to Lisa. "You. Get on the ship, female."

Lisa looks temporarily stunned, like she's just been hit by a Dom Bomb. Before she has a chance to comply, or rip his head off, he's already finished herding Shauna and Maggie onboard and is standing in the doorway looking back at her expectantly.

I lean in to whisper a few friendly words of encouragement when I feel a warm brick wall sidle up behind me. Freaking Lachlin. Not surprisingly, I forget what I was going to say to Lisa. Hell, I forget my name when I feel his heat on my back. It's a total hottie blottie meltdown. Brain. Shut. Completely. Off.

"You will join me on the bridge now, Amazon," Eff informs Lisa, and I find myself nodding on her behalf. I figure she's suffering from hottie blottie meltdown, too, so I try to help her out. What are friends for, eh?

Finally, she begins to nod slowly, too, mouth still agape. Yeah, I may be trespassing on a private moment between two star-crossed lovers, but I still can't look away. As I stand there wishing for a vibrator and some hot buttered popcorn, I feel that brick wall behind me start to shake. That's when I realize Lachlin is laughing, or trying with great effort not to.

Lisa is still standing there when an amused Lachlin leans over and whispers in my ear, "Come with me, Duchess."

The freaking shiver of all shivers courses through me, leaving me with goosebumps the size of Tarilean chipmunks. Stupid Lachlin laughs.

I toss a pathetic wave to Lisa and Eff and squeak out a quick "Later" as Lachlin presses his big, warm hand to my lower back, steering me toward the exit. I guess it's the exit. Are his fingers touching my ass? I don't really care. Lachlin's touching me. Brain. Shut. Off.

Outside, his hand slides away, and he almost seems to forget all about me as he cuts a path through the bustling crowds. Long lines of people snake around the weird alien cab stands, and a few weary travelers are boarding a large ground shuttle. Lachlin breezes right past them all, leaving me in the dust as he heads toward an elevated pedestrian bridge that leads back to the royal grounds. After the gulf between us stretches to about one Earth mile, he finally turns around to check on me.

Yeah, I'm pissed. He left me. Just took off and left me. This is exactly why I prefer nice gentlemanly suiters to hot, handsome, virile, studly sex gods like Lachlin. Did I mention handsome and narcissistic? Stupid Lachlin.

"Surely, you don't expect me to walk the whole way there?" Too late, I realize that my statement sounded more like a question. It wasn't.

Yes, the administration building, which is just a boring name for the king's palace, is next door, but it may as well have been on the other side of Pluto in these six-inch stilettos with platform fronts borrowed from Maggie. There's no freaking way I can trek through all those cobblestone and pebble-ridden ankle traps.

Lachlin pauses and begins a slow, purposeful perusal of my entire person. My girlie bits tighten at the heated look in his eyes, and suddenly, I'm Nippy McNippleson. All my instincts scream at me to fling my arms across my chest and hide the girls. Or, better yet, turn around, hail one of those alien death-traps they call cabs, and get as far away as I can from Lachlin MacTavish, professional slut slayer. But, do I listen? Of course not.

"What's the problem, Duchess? You too good to walk?"

Uh . . . Seriously? Suddenly, that nickname's not nearly as cute as I first thought it was. I prop a fist on one hip and hold out my leg, pointing my freshly polished toe at him. "I'm not exactly dressed for hiking, Lachlin."

Yeah, I've never been very good at smart-ass comebacks. I usually think of the perfect retort twenty-four to forty-eight hours later when I'm alone in bed.

Oh! By Jingo! His laser gaze targets my leg, tracking all the way up my thigh and disappearing somewhere beneath the hem of my short skirt. Is that him making that choking noise? My skin is on fire, my knees quivering like jelly molds, and my uterus is singing the second refrain to the Hallelujah Chorus when a freaking skyscraper presses itself into my back.

"You need a ride, pretty femki?" it whispers into my ear.

Huh? I whirl around, looking up to see a tall handsome Tarilean smiling down at me like I'm the last chip in a Pringles can. His arms are full of bags and packages as if he's just returning from a trip, and the muscles in his arms are bulging and on full display. Long blond hair, wavy and windblown, sweeps across the man's forehead, giving him a playful appearance, and his gorgeous violet eyes are enough to make a Jane Austen fan weep. So why, then, isn't he making my vagaga tap a happy dance the way it does with stupid Lachlin? It makes no damn sense.

"No, friend. She doesn't need a ride."

That rumbly, heavily-accented voice pulls my attention away from the handsome Tarilean, and I turn around to see Lachlin all up in my space. Surprise! Somehow, in the span of three seconds, his feet have eaten up the mile between us, and his big protective paw is resting on my shoulder. How the heck can I be both angry and turned-on at the same time? Appalled and pleased simultaneously? See? Totally confusing.

"No offense, *friend*, but why don't we let the little femki answer for herself?" The Tarilean flashes Lachlin a black look.

Uh oh. Sure, I'm a wee bit tempted to take the guy up on his offer just because Lachlin's being a bit of an ass, but I'm not stupid enough to actually do it. We certainly don't need to start a small civil war right now. Besides, what kind of person would I be if I dragged this innocent guy into my spat with the cranky Scottish sexpert over there?

"No, I'm fine. Really. But, thank you all the same." I smile and pat the guy on the arm. Then, I jerk my hand away quickly when I remember Tarileans don't view *touching* the same way humans do. At least, not between mackis and femkis. My bad.

He tilts his head, his expression going slack as little lines form between his eyebrows. Is he confused? I'm not sure how. I was pretty clear, I thought. Wait. How did Nordric teach us to say 'thank you' in Tarilean? My forehead crinkles in thought, and then, the answer comes to me like an epiphany.

"Hvali keetosh mak tzoomesk et adoreisce unse corpolesh." Proud of myself, I grin large and puff out my chest with pride. And that was my first mistake.

Lachlin's hand turns into a highly pressurized vise on my arm. The Tarilean's eyes take on a wild, hungry mien as they lock onto me, the same way a wolf might look at a cute little bunny. Then, he starts to growl. Freaking growls. At me!

"Well, fuck." Lachlin mutters.

What the hell? I take a few unsteady steps back, maintaining eye contact and holding up my hands with my palms facing out, very similar to how one might try to calm a rabid beast. "Wa . . . Wait a minute there, big fel —"

Suddenly, it's raining packages. They're everywhere, the sky, the sidewalk, the top of my head, and the Tarilean turns into a charging bull. I shriek and close my eyes, waiting for the impending collision, but then, a freight train hits me from the side instead. The station around me becomes a blur as I whiz past the unsuspecting crowd, sailing nimbly through the air right before I tumble headlong into a cushiony box about half the size of a small closet.

Somewhere behind me, a door swishes shut, a loud war cry echoes on a concrete battlefield, and a deep, gravelly voice with a thick burr rumbles, "Administration Building. Step on it."

Oh. My. God. I have always wanted to jump into a cab and yell that at the driver!

Anyway, I try three times to shove my skirt down over my ass before I realize I'm upside down and gravity's against me. Squawking, I frantically palm my bits and bobs as two big hands set me right again.

Once I catch my breath, I turn my attention to the hedonistic highlander beside me, still not sure whether to thank him or punch him in the damn throat. But after I see the look in his beautiful, murderous eyes, I decide it doesn't matter. Because this gorgeous Gaelic guy is about to kill me.

CHAPTER FIVE

Lachlin

It's been almost an hour, and Emily is still so pissed, she won't even look at me. I hate it, but even her cold treatment couldn't dampen my raging emotions when we first arrived back here at the administration grounds. I was totally beside myself.

Yes, I was an ass. Yes, I howled, beat my fists against the wall, and kicked at the concrete steps that led up to the castle. But in my defense, I'd never heard anything so fucking funny in my whole wretched life. It's lucky the sitter was already here by the time we arrived because neither one of us was really fit to take care of the babies tonight.

Now that we're leaving, I still have a painful stitch in my side from laughing so hard, and my stomach muscles ache like I've just done two hundred pushups. I pull myself together and stop hooting long enough to bark out a question.

"One more time, Duchess. Tell me how Nordric told Maggie to say 'thank you' in Tarilean?"

"No. I'm not saying it again," she huffs.

"Come on. Just one more time." I open the door and watch her climb into the back of the cab. Damn, her ass is a thing of beauty. I slide in behind her, rattling off our destination to the auto-pilot, and we lurch forward.

"Please?"

She tries to give me a stink-eye, so I shoot her my best, heart-melting sad little boy look, the one that always works on Aine.

She sighs and rolls her eyes. "*Hvali keetosh mak tzoomesk et adoreisce unse corpolesh*," she says. "He told her that's how she should always say thank you to him."

Fuck. I can't help it. I crack up, rolling around and slapping my hands against the side of the cab.

"Stop it," she snaps. "It's not funny. There's no telling what would have happened if you hadn't been there. I could have been raped. Or molested. Or killed, even!"

She has a point. I choke down the rest of my guffaws, wipe the tears from my eyes, and take a deep breath. "Okay. I'm sorry, Duchess. I just don't know whether to punch the guy in the face or fall down and worship at his feet."

"Well, I know which I'd prefer," she puffs. "Tell me again what it means. I want to be sure I get it right when I tell Maggie."

I bite down on my lips for a moment, trying to get myself under tight control before I repeat it. I know I can get through this one time with a straight face. "Okay. You basically said, 'Please allow me to show my naked gratitude by worshiping your magnificent body'. Or maybe it's 'worshiping your magnificent body naked.' I'm still not totally fluent yet."

She stares at me incredulously for a moment, and I manage to blink a few times while my facial muscles spasm and my lips jerk uncontrollably. Screw it. "Pffft."

Heaving a huge sigh, she reaches up and swipes her hands across her cheeks. She's either crying or I sprayed her with spit, but there's just no help for it. It's fucking funny. Bent over double, crying into my hands, I chortle all the way to the spaceport.

I manage to get it together long enough to pay the cab and escort Emily through the lobby. She seems twitchy as Hell for some reason, her head swiveling back and forth constantly.

"What are you looking for?"

"Him," she whispers dramatically. "I don't want him to see me again. Ever."

I press my lips between my teeth, forcing back any temptation to make light of the situation. Enough is enough. "He's gone, Duchess. You're fine now. Look. There's the shuttle."

With my hand against the small of her back, I lead her inside the sky-borne shuttle and hand our tickets to the conductor-bot.

"Please take any seat that is open," the bot says.

There's only about a dozen people total in the cabin, which looks like it could hold at least fifty with no problem. So there's plenty of room. My eyes settle on a couple of seats not too far from the auto-pilot console, and I head that way, Emily in tow.

She falls into one of them, fussing with the hem of her dress, which I somehow find too short and too long at the same time. I don't know why that surprises me. Everything about the duchess is a contradiction. Haughty, but sweet. Playful, yet serious. Innocent and naughty at the same time. She's a fucking riddle that I need to solve.

We barely have a chance to settle in before the cabin doors close and the ship's robotic voice instructs us to fasten our harnesses. While the prerecorded voice drones on giving the usual boring flight details, I glance around at the other passengers.

"*Attention, Passengers. Prepare for takeoff. We will reach* (pause . . . insert different voice) *Fisan Moon* (pause . . . resume first voice) *in exactly twenty point nine clicks, arriving at Gate Twelve of the* (pause . . . insert different voice) *Fisan Moon Megamall Complex, a wholly owned subsidiary of Tarilax Industries, Inc.* (pause . . . resume first voice). *Please be sure to gather all personal belongings before disembarking. Taroyal Cruiselines will not be not responsible for any lost or stolen items. We hope you have a pleasant visit. Thank you for choosing Taroyal Cruiselines.*"

Immediately, I feel the oxygen in the cabin begin to shift,

and I dig my fingers into the arms of my chair. I really hate traveling on public transportation. These shuttles are worse than the city buses used to be back home. With no more warning or fanfare, we slingshot forward through the bay doors with our asses plastered to the uncomfortable chairs. After a minute, the air pressure inside the cabin settles, my intestines somehow manage to untangle themselves from my liver, and we're on our way to the Fisan Moon.

"About time," Emily grumbles as she picks something off the too-high heel of her shoe. "Honestly, I don't know why we're even bothering. We've probably missed most of the dinner by now."

I don't respond, too preoccupied with the Aurelian mercs who appear to have ducked inside right before the cabin doors closed. They've taken a couple of seats right across the way from us and sit there quietly scowling. One of them keeps his hand tucked inside a thin claffer vest while the other seems lost in thought, his fingers sliding up and down a long barbed quill extending from his lower arm. With dread, my eyes subtly track the direction of their pointed stares.

At first, I thought they were ogling my duchess, and I have to confess, I was momentarily scared shitless. Would I have fought them? Hell, yeah. Would I have beaten them? I doubt it. Aurelians are natural born killers. Sure, I can hold my own in a typical fight, but these guys are anything but typical. I've never seen one less than seven feet tall and three hundred pounds. Needless to say, I was relieved as Hell when I figured out they were actually looking at the Tarilean male sitting on the other side of Duchess.

With my usual shrewd prowess, I observe the guy. He's older, probably mid-fifties, though it's hard to tell with these Tarileans. They don't age as fast as we do. Sitting there looking bored, his arms draped around a small backpack, there's nothing unusual that stands out about him. I look for any sign that he might be aware of the two mercs eyeing him from the other side of the transport, but don't find any. If he knows, he sure isn't showing it. The fucker is cool as a cucumber.

" . . . red or purple, I think. You didn't happen to notice, did you?"

I turn to blink at the duchess who hasn't stopped yapping since we took off. "What?"

She purses her plump pink lips at me and narrows those big baby blues. "You haven't heard a word I've said. Have you?"

No point trying to lie. I shrug and flash her my get-out-of-jail-free grin, the one that always got me off with murder when my mum was alive, and the one that's gotten me into more panties than an underwear model.

"Oh, don't even," she scoffs. "That might work on the bubble-headed bimbos you're normally with, but it won't get you anywhere with me, Mister."

Seriously? Could that be true? I may need to take a new approach with this hard-shelled beauty. For whatever reason, she doesn't seem to trust me, which makes her smarter than most, I suppose.

"Sorry. I'm not sure what it is about you, Duchess, but I find it hard to concentrate when we're sitting this close together." Gently, I trace the back of my finger up the outside of her thigh, pausing just beneath the hem of her dress.

A slow, sexy smile sneaks across her lips, and I'm about to pat myself on the back for a job well done when she launches the next torpedo at me.

"Lachlin MacTavish, you're so full of shit, your eyes are brown."

What the Hell? I've yet to meet a woman who could successfully withstand my amorous advances once my mind was set. Wait. Have I really set my mind on the duchess? The answer hits me like an Aurelian linebacker. Fuck yeah, I want her. I want her so bad, it hurts. Literally, like a fist to the balls.

I'm about to ramp up the charm, dazzle her with my rapier wit, and bowl her over with my stunning good looks when the Aurelians pick that precise moment to make their move.

The first one stands up, whips out a handheld molecular disbander from beneath his vest, and points it at the Tarilean beside Duchess. Some of the women and children begin to scream, including Duchess and at least a couple of the males. I wrap my arm around her, at the same time keeping an eye on the events unfolding around us.

The second Aurelian stays seated, but aims several dubious-looking quills in our direction. I pull Duchess closer to me, leaning as far as I dare in the other direction, trying my damndest to get us out of the line of fire.

"We don't care about you," the Aurelian with the quills tells the guy. "Just toss over the bag."

The Tarilean appears unfazed, that bored look still on his face. At this point, I drag the duchess onto my lap as discretely as possible and inch us further away in case one of the mercs makes good on a threat.

"Not going to happen, schlumper." The Tarilean tightens his grip on the backpack while they stare daggers at each other.

Well, hell. I happen to know for a fact that Aurelians don't like being called schlumpers, the term used for a cheap gun-for-hire with more brawn than brains. It's kind of like calling a thousand-dollar-a-night escort a hooker. These guys take pride in their adeptness at killing and always prefer the title *assassin* or *mercenary*. Besides, what idiot in his right mind would insult an Aurelian assassin who had a disbander and an armload of quills aimed at him?

"Is it really worth dying for, Tarilean?"

The Aurelian makes a good point, and I have to bite my tongue to keep from offering my opinion on the matter, too, which would be a resounding *no*. It isn't worth dying for, whatever it is.

"Pfft." The Tarilean laughs. "You tell me? Is it?"

The Aurelian looks baffled for a moment and then begins to lose his patience. "You have three clicks, then my buddy over here is going to start shooting."

"Go ahead," the Tarilean prods. "Just know that the disbander will deconstruct the bag and its contents right along with me. Then, you'll never get your hands on it."

Just our dumb luck. This Tarilean is fucking nuts, and he's going to get us all killed.

"Please! Just give it to them!" one of the Tarilean women pleads.

I'm pretty sure the Tarilean's going to die either way, but the honor code of their warriors demands that he protect his fellow citizens, especially the women and children. And he's definitely a warrior. Add to that the fact that I've never seen a crooked Tarilean warrior, and I know something weird is going on.

Regardless, I don't give two fucks about stealth or staying under the radar anymore. I just want to put some distance between us. So with Duchess on my lap, I scoot my ass over to the seat furthest away from the suicidal maniac.

"Then I guess I'll just have to put a quill right between your eyes." The Aurelian points at the Tarilean's head, and I suck in my breath waiting for the bloody finale.

"If you think you can do it before I press the detonator in my hand, go for it."

I glance down to see the Tarilean's fingers stuck inside a pocket of the backpack. Well, shit.

"You'd kill your own people by destroying the serum?"

"They're dead anyway if I let you take it," the Tarilean replies.

What the hell is he carrying in that bag? What serum?

"Lachlin," Duchess whimpers, her face burrowing into my neck.

Fuck. My heart squeezes in my chest, every cell in my body revolting against her fear. I have to do something.

There I am, totally focused on concocting some heroic escape plan, when a fuck-ton of quills heads our way. Tucking Emily beneath me, I make a wild dive toward the auto-pilot console. I have every intention of flipping over and taking the brunt of the landing myself, but I only make it half-way before I'm pounded by several little nails.

Duchess is screaming my name, but everything else is a tangled mass of confusion. It's chaos. There's a loud explosion, klaxons blaring, red lights flickering, people screaming. An ear-splitting roar rips through the cabin right before a massive, sucking tornado, and then we start to spin, flipping and turning, rolling and reeling until I think I'm going to throw up or pass out. I can't pass out.

"Duchess."

I'm squeezing her too hard. I know it, but I can't let go. She clings to me while I struggle to hang on to the auto-pilot console and drag us beneath it. My arms and legs strain to the point I think my muscles may burst. Then, finally, the cabin falls silent as we make it inside the tiny cabinet, and the winds stop trying to suck my lungs out through my throat. But we're still falling. And falling. And falling.

It feels like it's never going to end, never going to stop. Then, suddenly, it does.

Chapter Six

Emily

Ow. My muscles twitch, tricking me into thinking I can move my arms and legs. I can't. Dammit, I'm paralyzed. Every breath is a struggle, like I have a one-ton elephant camped out on my chest. Even my hair hurts.

I groan as my eyelids flutter open. Where the heck am I?

I'm in a box. A coffin? Surrounded by darkness—my heart begins to pound a tattoo that can't be anything but a precursor to a major coronary implosion. I need to calm down, focus on figuring this out one baby step at a time.

Okay. I know I'm on Tarilax with the rest of my crew. We've been here over a year now. We're supposed to go to a dinner party tonight. I have to pretend I'm on a date with Counselor Ja'Baal. The babysitter was late. I stayed behind with Lachlin. We boarded a shuttle to go to Fisan. We . . . Oh, God. Lachlin.

It's him. He's lying on top of me, two hundred and some odd pounds of dead weight. No. Not dead. He can't be dead.

"Lachlin," I whisper, not really sure why I feel the need to whisper in the first place.

He's alive. His steady breath on my ear makes me want to cry with relief. "Lachlin."

When he doesn't answer the second time, I wriggle around until I have one arm free. For reasons I don't even want to question right now, I run my hand up and down his side. I'm checking for injuries. Yep, that's what I'm doing. I'm definitely not feeling him up while he's unconscious because that would just be wrong. Right?

"Lachlin, wake up. We need to get out of here."

That's when I feel it. A quill. A fucking Aurelian quill.

Gasping, I carefully move my hand over the rest of his back and buttocks, counting at least five more quills poking out from his beautiful skin. I don't know how they all managed to miss me, but they did. Or, at least, I think they did, from what I can tell.

Didn't Lisa say the barbed tips were poisonous? Or, maybe the assassins put poison on them. Fuck. I can't remember now, and I sure can't think straight at the moment. I just know I have to get them out.

A spray of sparks hisses out from somewhere behind my head, and a slice of soft red light filters into our little cubby. Even with the light, all I can see is Lachlin, Lachlin's chest, Lachlin's shoulder, Lachlin's hair. He's everywhere.

"Lach. Lachlin!" I try shaking his shoulder, but it's no use. His breathing doesn't change, and he doesn't even twitch a muscle.

So I begin the slow task of slithering out from under him and trying to get free from this small cabinet he's somehow folded us into.

It's at least thirty minutes later when I finally pull my leg out through the tiny opening. I honestly don't see how he squeezed us in there in the first place, but I'm glad he did. It may have saved our lives. Now, I just have to figure out how to get him out of there.

I sit back, scratch my head, and sigh. I need a hand moving Lachlin. Peering out from behind the podium, I call out for someone, anyone to come and help us.

"Hello? Is anyone there?" No answer. Where is everyone? "Hello! We need help over here."

Oh, no. No, no, no. They're gone. Half the chairs, all the

people. Gone. There's not one person left onboard besides us. That's when I notice the rocking and the gentle sound of water lapping against the side of the craft. I reach back through the opening under the podium and place my hand on Lachlin's cheek.

"Stay here, Lach. I'll be right back. Don't move," I tell him.

Using the console to steady myself, I stumble to my feet and take my first good look around the cabin. Or, rather, what's left of the cabin. One whole wall is missing. Completely gone. It opens into a deep, dark void on the other side. I can't see a thing, but there's a hint of a warm breeze whispering across my face. It's easy to tell now that the cabin is rocking, and I can feel a warm, wet spray of water against my skin.

I glance back toward the spot where Lachlin lies. We're alive, and we're floating. Will we continue to float? Are we in a lake? An ocean? Is this Tarilax? Fisan? The other moon? Fuck! The questions are endless.

I walk around and study the rest of the cabin, hoping to find something I can use to get us out of here. But other than a few broken harnesses lying around, there's nothing else here. Not one thing. Not one person. Nothing.

All right. The cavalry's not coming, at least not any time soon. I have to do this myself. I can do this. First thing I need is a first aid kit. I walk around and check every nook and cranny until I find one. Thank God the medical supplies were mounted to a wall that's still intact. I open the small cabinet and take out the kit, praying there's something in it for poisonous Aurelian quills, knowing that even if there is, I won't be able to read the freaking label. Everything's written in Tarilean. Shit. I barely know half the Tarilean ABCs.

I'll figure that out in a minute. Right now, I need to get Lachlin out of the cabinet. I grab a pair of scissors out of the medical kit and cut away a harness from one of the remaining chairs. After putting it on Lachlin, carefully avoiding any quills, I use it to drag him through the gap and out to the open floor.

Please be okay. Please be okay.

Next, I paw through the Med kit, looking for something to remove the barbs from Lachlin's back. It's then I notice that water has started seeping through the open wall. We just can't catch a fucking break. I lift his face off the floor, my eyes darting around to find something I can use to prop his head. They settle on a seat cushion, which I rip out of the chair one-handed, then continue plucking out useful items from the kit.

I do my best to ignore the dark thoughts that eat at me as I attach a pair of forceps to the root of a quill. Even so, I can't do anything about the tears that are making my vision blurry. All those people, those women and children, gone. And for what? A few measly dollars? A stolen treasure? It's such a waste. So fucking unfair. I take a timeout, lift my face to the ceiling, and breathe deep. I'll fall apart later. Right now, Lachlin needs me.

"Okay, first things first, Fairchild. Get these damn needles out of him, then find a way off the ship. You can do this."

After my little pep talk, I bend down and take the forceps in my shaking hand. Holding them at a ninety-degree angle, I press my fingers against his skin and count to three before giving them a good sharp tug. I almost cry when the quill remains steadfast. I allow myself only a brief freak-out before I settle down and try it again.

Slap my ass and call me Judy! The quill comes out on my second try. I breathe in and out a few times, trying not to throw up as I study the barbed tip. The blood oozing from the wound looks black as it trickles down Lachlin's side. I press some gauze against it for a moment, then remove the quill from the forceps and toss it over my shoulder. Time to move on to the next one. Only five more to go. Fuck.

Once all the quills are out and I've doctored the wounds

with what I freaking hope is some kind of antibiotic or anti-septic cream, I'm ready to focus on phase two of what I'm calling my 'Oh God Don't Let Us Die' plan. It's a good thing, too, as the water on the floor is rising steadily, and there's not a candle's chance in Hell I can lift Lachlin's dead weight into one of those chairs.

Standing in the middle of the room, I turn around in a slow circle, using a critical eye to inventory everything at our disposal. Shit. There isn't much.

"Come on, Fairchild. Think. You have a gods damn degree in aerospace engineering. If anyone can do this, you can, for Pete's sake."

Problem is, an engineering degree is great if you want to build a spaceship on Earth. It's not so helpful if you're trying to rape and pillage an alien vessel in the dark to make a relia-ble watercraft. And, speaking of water, it's over my ankles now. I look down and see the seat cushion beneath Lachlin's head trying to float.

All right, there we go. Just like the aircraft on Earth, the seat cushions in the shuttle must function as floatation devices. Sheesh. I couldn't see the forest for the trees. In my panic, I was trying to figure out how to rip out the engines and rewire the electrical systems to create a freaking complex steamliner when the answer was so simple. Float.

In less than half an hour, I had every remaining seat cush-ion in the cabin ripped out and tied together with harnesses, electrical wiring, and something that looked suspiciously like coaxial cables. Now, we have something that could pass loosely as a raft. I pry off the backs of two chairs and toss them on the raft to use as paddles. It's not pretty, but it'll work. And that's all I can do. I drag the whole thing over to the missing wall and then go back for Lachlin.

Crap! Trying to drag Lachlin is like trying to haul a small Volkswagen with the emergency brake on, and really drives home the fact that I need to pee. Bad. I'll just distract myself with other things like Lachlin's hair, Lachlin's wide shoulders, Lachlin's cute round butt. All of which is in my face as I drag him onto the raft. It takes me nearly as long to get his limp, slack body onto the stupid thing as it did for me to build it. But I finally manage it, dammit.

With water up to my knees now, I load up what's left of the medical kit, a few of the extra wires I plundered from the console, and nearly a full bottle of water I found jammed in between two seats. Then, I push the raft through the missing wall and jump on.

Navigating the tenebrous environment is like fumbling through a Wes Craven movie set. It's creepy as Hell, and as the paddle slices through the black water, it doesn't take long to figure out that we're not in the middle of an ocean at all. Gauging by all the weird noises emanating from the surrounding banks, it's more likely a lake or a river.

At home, I'd be listening to cicadas, bullfrogs, maybe a few crickets right now. If I were really lucky, I'd even hear a hoot owl or the far-away call of a lazy coyote. That's what these noises bring to mind. But that's definitely not what they are.

This can't be Tarilax. If it weren't for the dim, red glow coming from the sinking ship behind us, I wouldn't be able to see my hand in front of my face. Tarilax has two moons, one of which is Fisan. Surely, one of them would be visible in the sky right now?

I don't know why it seems important to figure out where we are, but it does. Like to be in charge properly, to be able to take care of Lachlin the way he needs me to when he's this weak and vulnerable, I need to know. Everything seems so out of my control right now, and maybe just knowing where we are would give me back some measure of power, some small level of mastery over the situation.

I keep paddling, trying to remember how long we'd been

in the air by the time the shuttle exploded. We could be on Fisan, for all I know. Cora, Lisa, and the others could be having dinner not a mile away watching what they thought was a shooting star from the restaurant.

Ca-ca coo! Paaa-sheee-ka! Kill! Kill! Kill!

"What the fuck was that?" I freeze for a moment, then turn around and poke Lachlin in the butt with my finger. "Lach, wake up."

Nothing. He doesn't even twitch. So I do it again, hard, right in the crack this time so that the tip of my finger nearly breaches his butthole. Now, me? I could be in a coma, and that would have woken me right up.

"Lachlin! Naptime is over. Wake. Up." Still nothing.

I take a deep breath, and with shaky hands, start paddling again. "Stop being such a baby, Fairchild. It's just a few alien bugs. Nothing to get all worked up over."

Oonk-a-lunk. Oonk-a-lunk. Shuck-shuck-shukar-shukar. Tink-tink. Wee-bee. Wee-b-be-bee. Oonk-a-lunk.

Cocking my ear toward the sounds, I start paddling faster in the opposite direction. Then I stop, not at all sure that I truly want to get to shore any time soon knowing that's where all these creepy critters are.

Dick dick Fiss swee. Kill! Kill! Kill!

Okay, that's it. The last semblance of my sanity cracks, and I scream at the top of my lungs, "Shut the fuck up!"

THBBPTHBPT!

A raspberry? "Are you freaking kidding me?"

With all this stress, not knowing where we are, Lachlin still unconscious, surrounded by creepy smart-ass wildlife, not to mention all this water, I cannot ignore the fact that I have to pee any longer.

"There's no other option," I tell myself over and over as I pull down my panties, hang my ass over the side of the raft, and just let loose. *Ahh.* There is simply no better feeling in the world.

Well, until a deep, raspy voice rumbles through the darkness.

"What the hell are you doing, Duchess?"

Ker-plunk!

CHAPTER SEVEN

Lachlin

Fucking-A, that hurts. Something is definitely wrong here. I wake up wearing someone else's head that's about two sizes too small for my brain. My tired, limp body is floating around on a soft fluffy cloud, and someone has taken a cat o' nine tails to my back. I don't even want to speculate what's happened to my ass to make it sting so bad. Where am I?

It happens fast. Memories slam into my head with the force of a Boeing 747, and in the span of two tiny seconds, I remember everything. Yep. One second I'm lying here in a dream fog, and the next, every image, every explosion, every flying quill and crashing spacecraft plows into my brain like a locomotive, making it now four sizes too large for my cranium.

After a few tries, I manage to wedge my eyelids open a crack, only to find I still can't see. There's pitch black darkness all around me. Am I blind? Shit. Did I make it through the crash? Am I dead? Where's Duchess?

The sound of running water brings me to full consciousness, and I squint into the darkness. I think I feel more than see what I believe is Emily squatting beside me.

"What the hell are you doing, Duchess?"

Had I known what events that simple question would trigger, I might have held my tongue. But I didn't. So the next few seconds were confusing, to say the least. Fucking terrifying is probably a more accurate description.

First, Duchess lets out the shriek to end all shrieks, making my balls shrivel and my eardrums bleed. The next thing I hear is a loud kerplunk, followed by a hell of a lot of splashing and whooping and some pretty impressive cursing.

I try to get to my feet, quickly discovering that I have no balance at all, and whatever it is that I'm standing on is pretty damn set on tossing me off. I end up flopping back down on my ass, temporarily forgetting just how bad my ass hurts at the moment. This, of course, causes me to promptly join the creative cursing session that Duchess kicked off a few moments before. I finally manage to get ahold of myself, and I ease back down into a lotus position, taking a deep breath and focusing on the situation. It's more difficult than it should be.

My head is spinning. I mean, last I remember, I was on a spaceship plummeting to my death. Now I'm . . . Hell, I don't even know where I am. The River Styx? I reach up to scratch my head, and the next thing I know, Duchess magically appears on my lap. Instantaneously. Like she rocketed up from the bottom of the sea and materialized right here. I'll be the first to confess, I've thought a lot about having Duchess on my lap since we first met at the space station. But, never, in all those fantasies—and there were several—was she ever sopping wet and fully clothed. Both of which seem to be the case right now.

"Lachlin!"

"Duchess! What the fuck is going on?"

I want answers, and I want them now. I'm about to go all Lachlin-the-Dominator on her when she cuts me off at the knees. The little imp curls into me, her arms winding tight around my neck while her tender lips press into that sensitive spot right below my ear. Fuck, I melt into the soft, warm curves of her body.

"Oh, Lachlin," she whispers, her hot breath puffing against my neck and heating a streak of pure-grain lust that races straight to my cock.

Gods help me. That alone has my arms snaking around her, but then, she spreads her legs and straddles my lap, locking her legs around my back and snuggling into me so hard, I think maybe she's trying to crawl inside my skin with me.

"I was so worried." Her voice cracks. "You wouldn't wake up."

Oh, no. Is she crying?

"Please don't leave me again, Lachlin. Don't leave me," she sobs.

I sigh, knowing that I should be an expert at comforting crying women by now. Growing up in a houseful of females, it seemed like one of them was always either in tears or on the verge of them, especially with Bruce around. Hell, I've even given Eff lessons on how to handle situations like this. So why do I feel totally lost right now?

"Shh. It's all right, Duchess." I don't know what's happened, but she's scared to death and trembling like a leaf. If I had to guess, the way my body aches, I imagine it's been pretty bad. So I just concentrate on holding her for a while.

After a minute, I can't stand it anymore and break the silence. "Where are the others?"

She shakes her head, but says nothing.

Fuck. No one else survived? Out of all those people, only Duchess and I made it out alive? Maybe they left before we woke up? I mean, we were tucked into that tiny little cubby, hidden for all accounts and purposes. We could have been passed out and they just didn't see us. Were there any bodies at the crash site? Was there any blood?

I don't have the heart to ask her right now. In fact, I don't have the heart to even think about it anymore. Not right now. I don't have any more room for this guilt, not with all the other shit I carry around.

We stay this way for a long time, her crying in my lap, me trying to push away all negative thoughts about the crash.

Problem is, the only thing I have to replace them are sensuous thoughts caused by having Duchess straddling me.

I really do want to comfort her the way she needs right now. So, gently, my hand rubs circles on her back as I tuck her head beneath my chin. Rocking back and forth, I try to distract my dick by listening to the comforting sounds of the weird alien insects all along the banks. Except they're not really comforting at all. In fact, after a minute, they start to really creep me out. Those aren't exactly normal night-time noises.

"Hush now," I tell her. "I'm fine. Everything's fine."

She sobs and shakes, wiggling against me until I find it nearly impossible to ignore the fact she's there. Wiggling. In my lap. On my dick.

Yeah, my head hurts, my back feels like I've been whipped, my ass is sporting stab wounds, and just about every muscle in my body aches. But I'm fucking breathing. Therefore, my dick is hard as a rock. I reach down, no lie, with the purest intentions of repositioning her ass, when my fingers stumble upon a most interesting discovery. My little duchess isn't wearing any panties.

Where I come from, that's a clear deal breaker. I struggle with the predicament for about five seconds. I mean, in the best of times, the omission of underwear sends a clear message from the bearer, or non-bearer in this instance. In high-stress times such as this, the message is a bit hazier, a little less clear, but still communicates a definite theme, something like 'Come and get it, Big Boy.'

Being as attuned to the fairer sex as I am, there's no way I can ignore a message like that. Just as I'm getting ready to throw her down and rut into her like a sex-starved maniac, she leans back, sniffles, and grips my face between her hands.

"I was so worried about you, Lachlin."

Now, in my current state of mind, concussed with a hot, panty-less Duchess on my dick, the way my brain interpreted that statement was more like, "I want you to fuck my brains out, Lachlin."

Who am I to question the wishes of a duchess?

I attack her, launching a full-out assault on her lips, crushing them with mine, nipping, licking, and sucking. Fuck, she tastes good. Yeah, she might have squeaked a bit at first, but she's one hundred percent down with the plan now. Her fingers pull and tug at my hair, her tongue dueling in time with mine. I tighten my arms around her and pull her down hard against my lap, grinding into her so forcefully, I'm afraid I might lose my shit before I ever get inside her.

With her moans and whimpers fueling me, I have her flat on her back, her legs bent at the knees, and her dress pushed up around her neck in record time.

"Mm. Lachlin," she whispers, her hands fisting in my hair.

"Fuck, Duchess." I sit up, squinting and struggling to see her soft, naked curves in the thick darkness while my fingers scrabble at the buttons on my pants.

I've never been so turned on in my life. I'm fucking panting as her warm hands rub up and down my thighs, her nails scratching against the fabric as she whimpers and moans. I have to have her, or I honestly might die.

Finally, unbuttoned, unzipped, with my cock in my hand, I lean forward to drive it on home when, suddenly, there's a resounding thud that echoes across the water. The entire raft jolts and shimmies, and then falls away. I blink, and my duchess is gone. Gone, as in not under me anymore, and I'm airborne once again. Land fucking ho.

Thank God I hit the tree with my head and not my dick.

"Lachlin!"

Yeah, I don't respond. I just lie there on the shore, dazed with my dick in my hand as I close my eyes and contemplate life—Duchess, fate, karma, sand in my ass crack. Duchess. When I open them again, there are two big blue eyes staring down at me.

"Oh, my God! Are you okay?" She drops to her knees beside me, running her hands all over me. Except for my dick, of course, which she seems determined to avoid now.

"Yeah. I'm fine," I lie. Sitting up, I heave a battered sigh and put away my cock.

"Lachlin, you're bleeding again." Before I know it, she's back in my lap, straddling me once more and pushing back my hair while her fingers poke at a painful gash on my forehead.

Sure, I may be hurting, dying even, but again, I'm a man. She's in my lap. Straddling me. No panties. I groan as my fingers wrap around her waist, lift her off my still-hard dick, and place her gently on the ground beside me.

"Stay there." I point at the spot where she's kneeling. If she climbs back in my lap one more time, I fear she just might kill me.

One good thing I note as I glance around, whether it's because my eyes are adjusting to the dark or it's getting a little bit lighter, I can see. In fact, not only can I see Duchess, but I can make out a distinct shoreline in front of us and the sandy tapered bank we're lying on. Lifting my face to the sky, I also see why it's been so dark. We're on the only clear section around. Everything else is shrouded by an enormous canopy of trees. They're everywhere, even stretching out over the narrow channel of water we just came from.

I've been to Tarilax several times now, but I'm still no expert on the geography. I do know the Zaothe River winds through most of the harsh uncharted landscape, and like the Nile on Earth, covers more than four thousand miles from beginning to end. I also know that dense jungles surround most of the river and they are dangerous, even deadly. If that's where we are, we need cover.

The sound of something ripping grabs my attention, and I

turn to look at Duchess. Kneeling over her lap, she tears a long, thin strip from the bottom of her dress. When she's done, she holds it out in front of her, twining it through her fingers as she examines it closely.

"You're hurt," she explains. "I used most of the bandages in the first aid kit on your back and your . . . uh—"

"Ass?"

"Yep," she says, her lips making a popping sound around the word. She glances down at the shoreline and frowns. "Wait here a minute."

I watch as she jogs down to the water, grabs something off the raft, and jogs back. Dropping down beside me, she uncaps a bottle of water and pours a little over my wound. Then, she presses it to my lips and tips it so that I'm forced to take a drink. After a couple of good swallows, she takes it back, re-caps it, and stuffs it down inside the first aid kit between her knees. She scrapes her hand through the kit a few more times and pulls out a large tube of ointment, squinting at it as she squeezes a large green glob onto her finger.

"Now, if my Tarilean is correct, this should be antibiotic cream," she says as she stretches her hand toward my head. "Or antiseptic."

Uh. I don't think so. On reflex, my hand lashes out and snags her wrist. "Sorry, Duchess, but I'm not sure about—"

"About what? Getting an infection?"

I hate to sound chicken shit, but she really wasn't very re-assuring. I mean, what if that's not antibiotic or antiseptic cream at all? What if it's hemorrhoid cream? Or denture ad-hesive? Or toothpaste? Or hair removal? Not to sound con-ceded, but that cut is right beneath my hair line, after all.

She giggles as she peers into my panicked eyes. "Look, it's antibiotic cream, all right? You want to smell it?"

Smell it? "What the hell good would that do? I don't know what antibiotic cream is supposed to smell like."

She gives me a hard stare. "This is what I used on all your other cuts, too. It's hot out here, we're sweaty, and there's no telling what kind of alien germs are in that dirty water back there. There's too much risk of a cut turning septic out here. So, let go of my hand and suck it up, cowboy."

I take a deep breath and exhale slowly, making sure she knows I'm not thrilled about this. "Fine. Go ahead."

"Thank you." Gently, she dabs the cream to the cut on my forehead, her warm breath puffing against my cheek as she works. "Besides, if it was going to kill you, you'd be dead already. Right?"

Obviously, my duchess' bedside manner needs a little work.

CHAPTER EIGHT

Emily

Geez. Men are such babies. Still, my stomach tightens every time he winces.

"Almost done," I tell him.

He's so quiet, I glance down to make sure he's still breathing and notice his face practically nuzzled against my breasts. I bite down on my lip, trying not to laugh. Hey, whatever it takes to keep him distracted while I doctor his injury, I guess.

I finish up quickly, put away the cream, and pick up the long strip of cloth I tore from the bottom of my dress. This should take care of the bleeding even though it cost me another precious inch of hem that I really couldn't afford to lose.

"Now all I have to do is wrap it." I smile, trying to reassure him. Maggie would be so much better at this.

Carefully, I reach up and begin swathing the cloth around his head. Poor guy. He's got cuts and bruises all over him. I, on the other hand, haven't suffered even a little scratch. How did I manage that?

The answer hits me like a two by four. Because of Lachlin. Because of the way he hustled me away from the horny Tarilean at the space port, the way he edged me out of the path of danger on the shuttle, the way he covered my body with his when those quills were flying at us and backpacks were blowing up. And most importantly, the way he pressed me into that tiny cabinet so I didn't get sucked out into space after the explosion. Like all the others did. Shit. He saved me.

More than once.

Could I have been wrong about him? Maybe Lachlin Mac-Tavish is not the shameless libertine I thought he was?

On the last loop around his head, I tear the end of the bandage and tie it off. "There. All done."

Without overthinking it, I place my hands on his cheeks and lift his face. Then, I kiss him, right smack on the lips. No tongue, just my lips on his—those plump, fleshy, pouty, gorgeous lips of his that make my blood heat.

"What was that for?"

"Because I'm glad you're here with me?" I'm not sure why that sounded like a question. Or why I'm suddenly blushing.

"Truthfully, I wish neither one of us was here." He chuckles.

"Oh, well, yeah. Me, too. But if I have to be here, then I'm glad you're . . . you know . . . here with me, I guess."

Ugh. What am I, twelve?

He stands, brushes himself off, and helps me to my feet. Holding on to my hands, he gazes into my eyes for so long, I start to think he's going to kiss me again. And once I think it, I can't think of anything else. I want him to kiss me again. I freaking need him to kiss me again. I actually start leaning toward him, my face lifted, my eyes half closed, and my head tilting an invitation.

"I think it's the Zaothe River," he blurts.

"Huh?" I mean, I heard him. It was just an automatic response to a statement that was so far off the mark from what I was expecting, my synapses misfired. "Excuse me?"

He chuckles, his head dipping in embarrassment. "The Zaothe River. I think—" And then, he stops.

I wait for him to continue, my head bobbing forward in anticipation. "Yes? You think . . . what?"

"I think you're barefoot, Duchess. Where the hell are your shoes?"

Oh, yes. My shoes. I look around as if they might magically appear on the bank beside us when I know darn well they're somewhere at the bottom of the river. Oh, and those aren't the only things I lost when I fell in. Panties are so under-appreciated until you don't have them anymore.

I clear my throat, stalling so I can think of a way to explain this just right. One wrong word, and he'll want to know why I had my panties pulled down and my ass hanging over the side of the raft in the first place, and I'm damn sure not telling him about that.

I shrug nonchalantly. "I lost them."

"You lost them," he repeats, and I nod.

"Yes, in the river. Earlier, when you made me fall in."

"When *I* made you fall in?"

Okay. He's starting to irritate me now. I'm not sure why he's getting angry when I'm the one who lost a perfectly good pair of Jimmy Choos. It's not like I can run out and replace them for Maggie.

"Yes, when *you* made me fall in. You startled me."

"I startled you."

"Stop repeating everything I say!" Hand on hip, I scowl at him. I don't want to fight, but he's just so . . . so . . . *hot?* Irritating! "It's not like I fell in on purpose, Lachlin, and standing around arguing about it isn't going to help anything. I lost my shoes, and that's it."

He takes a deep breath and exhales loudly. "Right."

Seeming resigned to my stupidity, he walks back toward the river without another word, peering up and down the bank along the way. Then, he squats down beside the raft and starts pulling apart the floaty cushions.

What's he doing? I don't ask because I'm supposed to be mad. But I still want to know, so like any other normal red-blooded American woman, I pick at him instead.

"You know, it really doesn't matter, anyway," I muse

aloud. When he doesn't respond, I keep going a little louder. "It's not like I could have traipsed around out here in the jungle in high heels."

Of course, he ignores me, intent on his task, as if he doesn't have time to listen to me bitch about his unreasonable criticism. The wildlife symphony has started back up, or maybe it never really stopped and I just quit noticing when I was talking to Lachlin. I sigh, longing to hear just one normal sound, one tree frog or one night caller instead of these weird alien amphibian knock-offs.

Is he pouting? This is ridiculous. Well, two can play that game. I pick up a stick and poke little holes in the sand while I ignore him back, but the longer he's quiet, the more insane I get. I'm about to tell him how juvenile he's being when I hear the sound of ripping fabric. Naturally, being a curious creature by nature, I migrate toward the noise.

I watch him for a while, the muscles in his arms rippling across those broad, strong shoulders as he pries the cover off another seat cushion. He truly has an epic butt, round and firm, definitely squeezable. All in all, he's probably the perfect male package. At least physically. Makes me all tingly in my girly places.

"What are you doing?" My voice cracks, and I clear my throat.

He doesn't reply immediately, standing up instead while he studies a big scrap of material in his hands.

"Sit," he finally says, pointing at the ground between us.

Sit. Like you might tell a dog. Not 'Emily, will you take a seat here for a moment while I play with the seat cushions?' Or 'Won't you sit down and make yourself comfortable, Emily?' No, he just grunts like a caveman and points toward his feet. Sit.

Being the bigger person, I roll my eyes and sit. He flops down beside me, grasps my ankle, and jerks my foot onto his lap. Of course, I yip in surprise.

"Shh. You want every starving animal in the jungle to hear us?"

I don't even dignify that with a response. He's such a . . . meanie.

"What are you doing?" I ask for the second time. Of course, this time, I whisper.

He ignores me for the second time, too, holding my foot up in the air and wrapping the vinyl-polyester material around it.

"Shoes?" I take a guess.

"I don't know if you can actually call them shoes, but something like that." He scoffs as he secures the fabric to my foot using pieces of the harnesses. "Think that'll work?"

"Hm," I say, wiggling my foot. Then, I stand up and take a few steps. "Yeah, I think this will work."

After he finishes strapping on the second one, he climbs to his feet and watches as I test his new invention. Maybe they'll catch on?

"Thanks," I say as I clomp around the bank in my new foot covers, actually impressed though I'd never tell him that. Still, I think these will work tons better than my shoes out here.

And, that's when I hear a woman scream.

Rrrraaaaaahhhhhhh!

"What the fuck was that?" I screech from Lachlin's back where I've taken a running jump and latched onto like a baby sloth.

"Duchess," he groans. "My back—"

"Oh, shit." I drop back down to my feet, not letting go of his arm completely. "I'm so sorry. I forgot. I didn't mean to hurt you, but what was that?"

"It's just a bird or a frog or something."

A-ooooooo, wonk-wonk, kill! Kill!

I gasp, listening as something snuffles in the trees beside us. Lachlin stiffens beside me, which does nothing to put me at ease.

"Lachlin," I whisper.

"We can't stay here. We need to find cover somewhere until morning, someplace we can build a fire, stretch out, and rest." He narrows his eyes at the noisy trees and shrubs around us.

"Okay." I nod agreeably. That actually sounds great so long as I don't have to walk out there in the dark woods with those screaming, snuffling monsters waiting to ambush us.

"Where we going?"

"I'm not sure yet. Is the ship—"

"At the bottom of the river by now? Yes, I'm sure it is." I smile and bat my lashes at him.

"Then, we have no choice. We're going that way." He points to the woods.

When I don't reply, he locks his hands on my shoulders and physically turns my body in that direction. "Straight ahead."

I march to the edge of the clearing and stop, letting him go in front. If we're going to be eaten by a large jungle animal, he's got more meat on his bones than I do. They might even be full after they eat him, and I can get away.

He pauses at the wood line and turns around. "Follow me. And stay close."

Seriously? He thinks he needs to tell me that? Without another word, he takes off toward the trees, me following so close, I keep kicking the backs of his heels. We look like contestants in a three-legged race at the county fair as we push our way into the turbulent jungle.

"Try to stay on the path," he whispers.

Path? I look down at my feet, then at the overgrown wilderness around us. "What path?"

He ignores me, of course. We go on for a good while like this, establishing a decent rhythm—him walking in front, me walking so close, our feet often get tangled; him giving me dirty looks, me sweating and whimpering profusely. After a while, he pulls back a long branch and steps aside for me to go through. I squat, trying to keep my ass crack covered as a breeze blows up my skirt tail, and waddle about half-way through before smashing into a hard, furry wall with big fuzzy feet. Slowly, I lift my eyes, little gurgling noises coming out of my throat, when I see two big red eyeballs and a flash of fangs.

I quickly learn that my fight or flight instincts are defective, basically non-existent. Before I have a chance to scream, faint, run, or lose the contents of my bladder, two long, hairy arms snake forward, grip me around my waist, and yank me through the brush wall.

When I open my eyes again, we're standing in a little glade, surrounded by moonlight, and I get my first good look at my abductor. Now I'm not sure whether it's my help-me-I'm-about-to-die scream or the fact that I was wrenched away from him at the speed of sound that tipped Lachlin off to trouble, but I hear him crashing through the brush and shouting curses behind me. He's loud, and he's pissed, and I'm ready for him to kick this kidnapper's ass.

Peering into the face of the large porcupine-monkey beast who has a solid grip on my arm, I open my mouth to say something but can't seem to form any words. Its eyes drop down to my gaping maw, and it stares in fascination. Then, it reaches out a curious finger and pokes it in my mouth, gagging me and then tapping on my canines.

"Don't move, Duchess."

From the corner of my eye, I see Lachlin crouching like an NFL linebacker at the edge of the clearing.

"O-ay," I reply around the monkeypine's finger. "Ot oov-ing."

The big, prickly monkey looks at Lachlin and growls out a

warning, the long, needle-like quills on its shoulders wobbling and vibrating. At the same time, it pulls me closer and shuffles us further away from Lachlin.

"Lachlin," I squeak. "Do . . . something."

"That's a monipher," he says coolly, as if classifying the fucking thing is going to somehow help me. Suddenly, I want to slap the shit out of both of them.

Fortunately, the monipher stops shuffling before we hit the tree line behind us, but far enough away from Lachlin that it doesn't feel threatened anymore. At least, that's what I'm guessing. But, unfortunately, that's when it seems to take a renewed interest in me.

A very, very renewed interest.

Chapter Nine

Lachlin

That horny monkey has Duchess in a death-grip, squeezing her tit like a stress ball. I'm so pissed, my hands curl into fists. I mean, *I* haven't even gotten to squeeze her tits yet, and this simian skirt-chaser is over there busting a nut.

"Try talking to him," I tell her as calmly as I can.

It won't do anyone any good if we lose our heads here. Besides, if Duchess distracts him, maybe I can sneak close enough to make a grab for her. I'm afraid if I rush them, he'll take off into the jungle and disappear with her, and I might never find her again.

"Stop that!"

I look up just in time to see her drop the first aid kit on the ground and slap his hand away. She fucking slapped the killer moniper. My jaw drops open, and I stare with wide eyes as he bares his teeth and growls at her.

"Uh . . . I meant talk to him in a soothing way, Duchess, not pick a fight. Maybe you should try apologizing and then not hitting him again."

"Maybe he should try keeping his damn hands off my boobs," she snaps.

The moniper snarls and makes a familiar whining noise, the same one I made not long ago. I know just how he feels.

"You can throw a fit all you want," she snipes. "But I'm not going to stand here and be molested by a fucking monkey."

Geez, we're screwed. After a little more rumbling and

snapping, by both of them, the monipher moves on to explore Duchess' face, her hair, her arms, and her hands. At my urging, she stands still, letting it investigate what no doubt is its first look at a human, and I start to think that maybe we'll all get out of this alive. But when curiosity gets the better of him, he reaches down and yanks up the bottom of her skirt.

Fucking Hell.

Everything after that happens so fast, I barely have a chance to process it. There's screaming, growling, cursing, a loud crack, and a furious howl. I catch flashes of Duchess' ass, sharp teeth and fangs, a fist flying through the air, a monipher's ass. Did I mention Duchess' ass? The monipher lets out a wail so loud, so bloodcurdling, I nearly shit my pants. Then, he does a backflip, kicks a tree, and tears off into the jungle like a striped-ass ape.

"What the—" I fall over my feet trying to get to Duchess.

"Lachlin!" She throws herself at me, clinging like a wet towel to a rusty nail. "Oh, my God. Is it gone?"

I tighten my arms around her as she buries her face into my chest. "Yeah, sweetheart. It's gone."

She feels so good pressed into me like this. I give her a few minutes to calm down and stop trembling while I try to purge the image of her plump, round perfectly formed ass from my mind. It's no use. It's branded on my brain. In fact, if I run into that perverted monipher again, I should probably thank him for giving me the extra fuel for my spank bank.

"Come on, Duchess. Let's get out of here."

She nods her little head against my chest, sniffling as she scoops up the first aid kit and ambles back toward the trees. "Yeah. Let's go."

This time, I grab her hand and hang on tight. I'm not going to risk losing her again. I press forward with the duchess in tow, beating a new path between tree trunks as wide as Buicks and through every kind of brush and shrub imaginable—big orange bushes, little yellow scrubs, prickly cactus-like plants, scary Venus Flytrap hybrids, and even one that looked a whole lot like Abe Lincoln, the younger years. They poke and claw at our skin, tear at our clothes, but even that's not as bad as the snarling, rustling noises of unknown origin coming from the thick undergrowth around us. I don't know whether to be glad we can't see them or not, but it keeps Duchess on edge.

"I think they're getting closer," she whispers, her head whipping around in every direction.

"They're not."

"They're watching us, looking for weaknesses, and waiting for the right moment to pounce."

"They aren't."

"What do we do if they attack us?"

"They won't."

Honestly, they might, but I can't very well tell her there's a good chance we're going to be mauled or eaten alive by a lionuffalo. Or a sheeta. Or any of the other hundreds of Tarilean predators I don't know the names of.

My reassurance seems to make her more at ease. Or she's just decided to stop voicing her concerns since I keep dismissing them. Either way, she's quiet until we reach a steep incline that stretches in both directions as far as my eyes can see, which really isn't that far since it's still dark.

"Great. It's the grand canyon of Tarilax."

"It's not that big." I chuckle at her dramatics.

Resting my hands on my hips, I weigh the better option—climb it or walk around it. I don't know how far it stretches, but the landscape is not very inviting in either direction. If it were just me, there'd be no question, but I have to consider Duchess. She's in pretty good shape. I think she can do this. Actually, I'm sure of it. It's more like a big hill than a mountain, anyway. It's definitely scalable.

"I think we can climb it," I tell her casually. "You go first. Just be careful. That blue Tarilean mud is slippery."

She crosses her arms and gives me a hairy eyeball.

I arch my brow back at her. "What?"

Maybe she doesn't know how to climb, or she's afraid of heights?

"I'm not falling for that," she says. "You go first."

I'm confused for a moment, and then, it hits me. She's not wearing underwear. I couldn't stop the naughty smile from stretching across my face if I wanted to. "You have to go first, Duchess. If I slip, I'll take you down with me. If I land on you, it'll probably kill you."

She thinks for a moment, then snipes, "Fine. But you have to give me a good head start. Wait 'til I'm at least half-way up before you start climbing."

"Fine. Go."

She stands there staring until I wave my hand at the cliff impatiently. "Well?"

"I don't trust you," she boldly admits. "Promise me you won't look."

I will promise no such fucking thing. I have every intention of looking as hard as my eyeballs will let me. I huff and roll my eyes as if the accusation is totally offensive. "Will you just go before one of those animals we've been hearing decides to come over and get a little midnight snack?"

Okay, it was a cheap shot, but it works. She places a seat-covered foot into the dirt and reaches out for a good hold. Then, she gives me one last look over her shoulder.

"Turn around."

I sigh, shaking my head and giving her my back. And, because I'm so gallant, I wait until I'm sure she's gotten at least one good leg up before I turn around.

"Is that how you knew we were still on Tarilax? Because of the blue mud?"

Her silky, sweet voice spills down the side of the hill, and I have to crane my neck to see her. It's more than worth the effort, though. Her creamy white ass is shining in the Tarilean moons' light. I could see so much better if it was daylight, though.

On the serious side, she appears to have a solid grasp of the terrain around her, and she's scrambling up with ease. With her toned body and her military background, I didn't really expect her to have any problems. But, she climbs like a professional.

"Actually," I call up to her. "It never occurred to me that we'd be anywhere else other than Tarilax. Where did you think we were?"

She's not near the half-way mark yet, but I go ahead and start climbing anyway, lured by the view from beneath her skirt.

"I wasn't exactly sure, but I was leaning toward Fisan," she says. "Seemed like we'd be closer to there than Tarilax."

"That makes sense, but we would've probably been dead by then if we'd landed on Fisan. The planet isn't fully terraformed yet. Plus, there's the fact that all shuttles are preprogrammed to return to the spaceport in an emergency."

I catch up with her in no time, not because she's a poor climber — she's not — but because my arms and legs are twice as long. I have to say, too, that flashes of her ass in that skirt are fucking inspirational, a great incentive for me to climb faster. Hey, I never actually said the words 'I promise not to look.'

It's that round, jiggly ass that I'm focused on when she reaches for a shallow pocket in the cliff face. Her fingers grip the dimples perfectly, and she hangs on with no problem as she releases the other hold. But as soon as she lets go, I feel a shower of dirt and tiny pebbles stinging my cheeks. Then, I hear the fracturing of rock and her loud panicked gasp.

"Lach—"

I throw my arm up just in time to catch her, bracing her entire ass in one hand, but not before a chunk of broken slate glances off my cheekbone. Biting back a curse and squeezing her ass cheeks like a roll of Charmin, I press her into the side of the ravine.

"Got it?"

"Yeah, I got it," she says, hugging the cliff with her entire body.

Thank fuck. Reluctantly, I remove my hand from her ass and use it to swipe at my cheek. Blood, and lots of it. I can feel it dribbling down my chin, dripping onto my chest. It's impossible to tell how bad it is without seeing it, but at least, I know it's not life threatening. I mean, no one I know has ever died from a cut to the cheek. Now, a scar? That's more likely. Question is, how big will it be, and will it make me look ruggedly handsome or horribly disfigured?

Duchess reaches the top of the cliff and scrambles over the side. A second later, her head pops back over the edge, followed by her hand as she offers to help me up. As if.

"Fuck a duck!" she suddenly screeches, startling me so bad, I nearly lose my grip and fall back down the hill.

"What the hell?" I shout back just as my head pops over the top. Using both hands, I grip the ledge and grunt while I pull up the rest of my body.

"You're bleeding again!" she says, as if I'm only doing it to spite her. "What did you do this time?"

"What did *I* do?" I frown at her.

"Come here and sit down." She grabs me by both arms and shoves me onto a large boulder, totally ignoring my question. From the way she slaps the first aid kit into my hands, I rightfully assume she wants me to hold it while she stirs everything around inside.

"We don't have any bandages, but there's more of that

antibiotic cream. Here, hold this." She pushes a tube of cream into my hand, removes the bottle of water, and sloshes it around, weighing the contents. Then, she tears off the lid, presses the bottle to my lips, and says, "Drink."

So I do.

"This is all the water we have until we find some more. I need the rest of it to clean your wound," she informs me as she pulls it away.

I swallow and then frown at her. "I thought that's what the antibiotic cream was for?"

"To clean your wound? It is, but I have to wash all the dirt out before I can put any medicine on it."

Before I can respond, she's angled the water bottle in front of my face and squirted half of it into my cut and the other half into my eye. Then, it's gone. All of it.

"What the hell, Duchess?" I have a kit in one hand and a tube of cream in the other, so I couldn't grab her hand to stop her.

"What? Did that hurt?"

"Hell no, it didn't hurt. I don't care about that. Why didn't you at least take a sip before you sprayed the rest in my face?"

She's been out here walking as long as I have. She has to be thirsty, too. It's not unbearably hot, but it's muggy enough to work up a sweat, and we've been at this for a while now. It occurs to me that I don't much care for the thought of her going without for me, either. Hell, I don't like the thought of her going without for anything, especially me.

"I wasn't thirsty," she says.

Lie. I can tell by the way her eyes dip down and the tip of her tongue peeks out to lap at her lips.

"Besides, there was barely enough left to rinse your cut. I'll be fine until we get some more."

I clench the tube of ointment in my hand, trying to keep from throttling her. Or hugging her. I'm not sure which.

"Anyway, it's done now. Hand me the cream."

I slap it into her open hand, probably a little too hard, but she doesn't say anything. She just gives me an icy look while she opens the cap and squeezes a generous amount onto her finger.

Studying my wound through squinty eyes, she dabs the medicine all over it. Finally, she sighs and wipes her fingers on her dress. "Well, there goes that pretty face of yours. You're going to have a scar. You really need stitches."

I only heard one part of that whole dialogue. "You think I'm pretty?"

I can't tell for sure in the moonlight, but I think she blushes. "Well . . . I mean . . . Yeah. You know you are."

"I know *you* are. Me? I've damn sure never thought of myself as pretty. What man wants to be pretty?"

She shrugs, an action that conveys any number of sentiments, such as 'tough shit' or 'it is what it is' or 'get the hell over yourself.' She cups my chin in her hand, gently turning my face this way and that, and I'm not sure if she's examining my cut or just debating my looks.

"I wish we had sutures, but I'd settle for a bandage right now," she finally says.

My eyes immediately flick to the hem of her dress, and I damn near start panting. Could I be so lucky? One more rip along the bottom, and her dress will look more like a shirt. And with no panties? Her entire succulent pussy will be on display.

"Don't even think about it." She laughs, knowing exactly where my wicked thoughts have wandered.

"Can't blame a guy for dreaming, sweetheart."

"If I rip any more off the bottom of this dress, your dreams are probably gonna come true pretty quickly."

I give her my sexiest grin. "Well, like you said, we don't want to take a chance on the wound going septic, do we?"

CHAPTER TEN

Emily

And, that's why Lachlin is missing the bottom part of his shirt. Septicemia is no laughing matter. It had nothing at all to do with the fact that now, his stomach—his flat, taut, six-pack-laden stomach—is fully exposed for my viewing pleasure. Unlike him, I would never be that shallow or stoop that low. So what if I've stumbled a couple of times—all right, four times—because I can't seem to keep my eyes on the path? That's only because I'm tired.

"You tired?"

"Nope." I shake my head for further emphasis. "Nuh uh. Not a bit."

What the heck is wrong with me? This is not an endurance contest. Why didn't I just admit that I was tired? We've been walking around for at least two hours without a break, my mouth feels like I've been sucking on cotton balls, and my feet are sweating like nuns in a cucumber patch.

But I know why. Because I didn't want him to think less of me. That's why. I don't want him to think I'm weak. I want him to think I'm Superwoman, but why the heck should I care? Why do I care what Lachlin MacTavish thinks of me?

"We need to find some water soon," he says, making me lick my lips with my bone-dry tongue.

Boy, is he telling me!

"Do you even know where we're headed?"

He better. Because to me, it looks like we're walking

around in circles.

"Narsi," he replies.

"Pardon?"

"North. Narsi means north in Tarilean. See that constellation?" He points to a cluster of stars in the sky.

"Yeah?" I really don't. I just see a bunch of stars.

"Well, that's Urgowa's Children."

"Say what?" I laugh. "You just made that up."

He shakes his head. "No, really. That's what the Tarilean's use as their North Star."

"Who's Urgowa?"

"Urgowa, according to Tarilean legend, was the goddess of . . . fertility or some shit."

"Nice." I scoff, shaking my head at his storytelling skills. No one will ever accuse him of waxing poetic, that's for sure.

"Anyway, this goddess, Urgowa, is supposed to have given birth to all life on Tarilax."

"*All* life? Like bacteria and amoebas, too?"

"Now you're just being silly." He chuckles, then looks reflective. "But, maybe. Urgowa literally means 'mother of life' in Tarilean."

"Seriously? What happened?"

"True story," he says, grinning sweetly. "Millions of years ago, this Urgowa chick was floating around the cosmos, or whatever goddesses did back then, when she came across Tarilax. It was so pure and beautiful with its natural landscapes, lazy rivers and uncorrupted wilderness that she had to stop and take a closer look. That's when she met this god dude named Qake."

"Cake? Cake, the god? Was he German Chocolate or Italian Cream?" I giggle at my own joke because, well, I'm a nerd, and we do that. "Did she get her Qake and eat it, too?"

"Apparently." He laughs.

We keep walking, and I'm waiting on him to finish the

story, but he doesn't say anything else, and I'm determined not to ask him. I try to think of other things to get my mind off it. I whistle, I hum, I tap the Star-Spangled Banner with my thumb against my hipbone. I even make several attempts to touch the tip of my nose with my tongue. Finally, I can't stand it anymore.

"Well?" I snap.

"Well what?"

"Well, there has to be more to that story, Lachlin. What happened to her? Did she and Qake get together? Did they live happily ever after? Or did she end up choking him to death for starting stories and not finishing them?"

His face goes slack. He blinks a few times and shrugs. "I don't really know. Eff didn't tell me all of it, and it was a long time ago. Honestly, I think we were high at the time. There was something about a storm, Qake died, and her children got scattered all over the universe."

Good grief! I just stare at him in disbelief, words completely escaping me.

"Oh! And tears. She cried seven teardrops."

"Seven?" I repeat, because really? "Only seven? Not eight?"

He chuckles. "Just seven."

I don't even bother asking anything else. He's right—he was most likely stoned when Eff told him about it, or had his head up some girl's skirt in typical Lachlin fashion, or so I've heard. Besides, I don't go in for all that romantic bullshit, anyway.

The real story is probably more like Urgowa was on vacation eating cake when she stopped for directions on Tarilax and fell for a sexy gas station attendant named Larry who fucked like a god and who'd probably never heard of contraception before. Seven years later, Larry skipped town leaving Urgowa with seven kids. I mean, she was a fertility goddess, right? Larry probably could've shaken his pecker at her and knocked her up at least once a year. After giving birth to the last one, Urgowa probably cried for seven years. I know I would have.

Suddenly, Lachlin freezes in his tracks. He flings his hand out and grabs my arm, placing a finger to his lips. "Shh!"

Oh, God. What kind of two-headed, four-eyed, horny, purple people-eater are we dealing with this time?

"What is it?" I whisper.

"Shh. Listen." He cocks his ear toward a particularly dense copse of trees and stares straight at me. His eyes pose the silent question — *Do you hear that?*

I tilt my head, too, straining every otolaryngological muscle I possess. Nothing. I frown and shake my head, giving him a silent response to his unspoken question — *I don't hear jack.*

"Water." He smiles. "This way."

He jogs off through the trees, tugging me along behind him. Well, dragging me along behind him. Definitely dragging.

We don't go very far before I hear it, too. The delicious burbling of water, lots and lots of water. My feet get a little more energetic, but when the path disappears into a thicket of colorful fauna, I nearly cry. Disappointed, I watch as Lachlin peels back a cluster of ginormous purple elephant ears. And there it is, the Holy Grail of hidden paradises. I can't believe my eyes.

"Holy schnizzle!"

"Fuck me," he murmurs. "It's one of the tears."

"One of the what?"

"Urgowa's tears." He smiles, his eyes locked on the scene in front of us. "It's one of the seven sacred pools. It's supposed to have miraculous healing properties or something."

Call me crazy, but that's kind of a big fucking detail to leave out of the story. I don't dwell on it, though. It's impossible to stay irritated as we stand there on the adjacent plateau, watching in awe as water bursts through the trees, spills out over the cliffs, and crashes into a perfect plunge pool below.

The water looks almost turquoise in the moonlight, with rainbow-colored dragonflies the size of pixies skimming across the top. The pool itself is crystal clear, and even from here, the underwater rock formations are visible. They're practically luminous, like there's a light installation at the bottom of the pool. To top it off, this secret Garden of Eden — or sacred tear of Urgowa, if Lachlin's to be believed — is shrouded by purple palms, blue and yellow shrubbery and tropical orange woodlands on every side.

"Ready?" he says with all the excitement of a child on Christmas Eve.

"Oh, yeah."

"Come on. Let's go check it out."

He's already making his way down the ridge before he finishes the sentence, all caution to the wind. His enthusiasm is contagious, and I skip along behind him like a lovesick teenager. Thank goodness this climb isn't anything like the last one. Within minutes, we're standing right beside the falls.

"Do you think we can drink it?" I try to keep the desperation out of my voice as I watch Lachlin scoop water directly from the fall.

In response, he slurps a mouthful out of his cupped hands, sloshes it around in his mouth, and swallows. "Ahhh."

Then, he gets some more.

"Here. Drink," he says, offering the next handful to me.

No thought necessary. I pucker up and slurp until there's only a minuscule drop left in the palm of his hand, then I lick that off, too.

"More," I pant.

If someone had told me yesterday that Lachlin MacTavish

would have me eating out of his hands, I would have laughed in their face. Yet, here I am, tonguing his palm like a cow on a salt lick. I don't care. I was so thirsty, I would have lapped it out of his belly button.

"Is it just me? Or is this the best fucking water you've ever had?"

I nod enthusiastically. "I don't even know how to explain it. I've never tasted anything so fresh, so invigorating in my life."

After we've drunk about half the lagoon, we sit down on the lip of the pool and plop our aching feet into the cool, refreshing water. I feel better immediately. Power of suggestion? Maybe. He says the water's magic, therefore, I feel its magical powers flowing up through my toes. That's too nerdy, even for me.

I forget about superstitious alien voodoo and everything else when Lachlin wraps his arm around my shoulders and pulls me into him. We sit there quietly staring at the waters, hypnotized by the beauty of it.

"Lachlin?"

"Yeah?"

"How'd you get here?"

He's quiet for a second, then chuckles. "Maybe you've forgotten already, but I was on the same shuttle as you when it blew up."

"No. Not here. I mean *here*."

"Well, that clears it up."

"Here on Tarilax. In space," I add hastily.

He stops breathing. His body tenses, and his arm tightens around me. Well, crap. I've screwed up. I've crossed a line, one that I didn't even know existed. But I never thought it would be that bad. Not from what Aine said, anyway. According to her, he was taken by a rich, beautiful empress, supposedly the most beautiful woman in the whole freaking universe. Aine said she worshiped and adored him, basically idolized him. That doesn't sound like Hell to me. What warm-blooded, over-sexed human or non-human male wouldn't love to have a gorgeous, powerful, sensual slut fawning all over him twenty-four seven?

"I'm sorry, Lachlin. Please, just . . . forget I asked." I try to sit up, but he tugs me back against him.

"No, *I'm* sorry, pet. It's just that I haven't really told anyone about that," he says. "Not the whole story, anyway."

"Not Eff?"

He shakes his. "No."

"Not even Aine?"

"Especially not Aine." He blows out a breath, his eyes glazed as he stares at nothing. "Believe me, it's not the kind of story you share with your little sister."

Uh . . . wait. If they're that bad, I don't think I want to know, either. For some reason, that really chaps my ass, too. I find the thought of Lachlin and that *woman*, actually any woman, morally and spiritually repugnant. And apparently, physically repugnant, too, because my stomach is rolling and churning, and I suddenly want to retch.

This is so confusing. I mean, why the heck do I care what they did? I barely even like Lachlin. He's hot, yeah, but he is so not my type. I don't care what he does or who he does it with. Do I?

Shit. I'm sorry I asked now. I don't want to think about it anymore. I'm just going to wipe it totally out of my mind. Not another word about it. Nada.

"But, I think I want to tell you," he says. "For some reason, I want to tell you everything."

"Okay."

Brain. Shut. Completely. Off.

CHAPTER ELEVEN

Epherus

I place my hands on the Pelophesian marble countertop at Taroyal Cruiselines and trace the silver swirls of the grain with my finger. This countertop alone probably costs as much as a fully-loaded shuttle. Some call it conflict marble. I call it blood marble. Whatever you call it, with more than three-quarters of the universe's marble quarries still under the control of the Pelophesian military government, it's mostly illegal to sell or trade.

There's no telling how many slaves had to die or how many bribes the executives here at Taroyal Cruiselines had to pay so that we could admire the prosperity and prestige of their fine organization. I guess that's how big conglomerates like them operate. Though, I'm a little confused that they can apparently afford blood marble countertops, but they can't shell out enough cash to have working trackers installed in all of their passenger shuttles.

I leer at the greasy little case worker who's been assigned to our missing persons claim. He's been dodging our questions and giving us the runaround for nearly two hours now. We've filled out so many forms, I'm starting to think it's a delay tactic. Every time we ask something he doesn't like, he suddenly remembers a new form we need to fill out. They're on the case, he told us. Let them handle this, he said. Like fuck. I want the godsdamned passenger list for that shuttle, and I want it now.

"Look," the minimum wage shuttle agent sighs as if I'm wearing on his patience. "Like I said, I'm terribly sorry, Mr. Zinto, but I'm afraid that information is protected under the Universal Trade Commission Intergalactic Privacy Act. You really should just go on home and wait—"

"Stop!" I shout, unable to control my anger a moment longer, and truthfully, getting off on the way he nearly jumps out of his skin every time I growl at him. I know I promised Lisa that I wouldn't kill anybody while we're here, but this guy has used up all my restraint. "You will give me that passenger list, along with the ship's last known coordinates, or I will rip your balls—"

"Eff!" Lisa snaps.

I growl at the oily bastard, making a point to show him my impressive fangs and long sharp quills before prying my eyes away to look at Lisa. My poor little Amazon is exhausted with worry. I hate seeing those dark circles beneath her beautiful green eyes, or those deep lines etched into her forehead. With Emily and Lachlin missing, she's the glue holding their friends together. Her anxiety is nearly palpable, and I don't like it. I don't like it one bit. I feel helpless. I need to kill something.

"Maybe you better let me handle this," she says, conjuring a little smile as she pats my hand.

Lisa turns to face the shuttle agent and leans forward to rest her buxom breasts on the countertop between them. She folds her arms, pressing those magnificent melons together and causing the mouth-watering mounds to swell and nearly pop out of her low-cut uniform top.

"Listen, Mr . . ."

"Pettitfoure," he pants. "Patombre Pettitfoure. You can call me Pat," he says to her tits, breathy and practically salivating on them.

"Uh . . . Okay, then. Pat."

She says his name as if they're all but fucking, pausing for a moment afterward like she's wrestling with an idea. Or an upset stomach. Or maybe she's just giving him time to finish jizzing in his shorts the way he's drooling over her tits. Whatever. I don't like it.

I have to grit my teeth when she reaches out her hand, places it next to his on the counter, and wiggles her fingers at him. He swallows so loud, it echoes through the empty office, then he slides his greasy hand into hers.

What the hell? I know what I promised Lisa, but I'm going to have to kill this little fucker before we go. I just don't see any way around it.

"So, Pat," she coos. "I'm really sorry if we're being a pain. It's just that we're crazy worried about my . . . sister. You have to understand, my sister . . . my *twin* sister is out there somewhere all by herself, probably cold and scared to death. Her life could be in danger."

My eyes narrow as I watch the little thespian push out a couple of big crockapotamus tears. She shakes her head and sniffles.

"I'm sorry. It's just the thought of my little sister — er, my twin sister out there in the wilderness alone and shivering, fighting for her very life is almost too much to bear. And, Pat . . . there's absolutely nothing I wouldn't do to get her back. You know what I mean?"

I think he's going to hyperventilate, but somehow manages to blink out of his lusty daze long enough to nod and clear his throat. With a shaky hand, he passes her a tissue, then places his hand on her arm, giving it a little squeeze.

Slowly. I will kill him slowly.

"Well, my dear, you'll be relieved to know that it rarely ever gets below eighty degrees farkleheight this time of year. And I thought you said she was traveling with a . . ." He trails off, letting go of her long enough to pick up one of the one million pieces of paper lying around. Humming to himself, he drags his bony finger down the page until he finds the information he's searching for. "Ah! There it is. Lachlin MacTavish?"

Lisa drops her hand from her face, forgetting about the tissue and the fact that she's supposed to be crying as she gives him an icy stare. For one fleeting moment, the frown on her face perfectly conveys the actual depth of her disgust and displeasure with the little creep. Then, she jumps back into character, dabbing at her nose with the tissue and sniffing.

"Well, yes. She is, but she doesn't have her asthma medicine with her. And she simply can't breathe without it, not when she gets anxious or excited. She could asphyxiate at any time."

She releases a loud sob into the tissue and dabs at her nose. The little bastard frowns, then places his hand on hers, nodding sympathetically.

"Or her diabetes medication," Lisa adds, her eyes soft and glistening. She flutters her damp lashes and leans in closer to him. "In fact, she was on her way to the pharmacy to refill her insulin. Without that, she'd need to have chocolate or something sweet to regulate her blood sugar. She could have seizures, go into shock, even lapse into a coma. She could die, Pat! Surely, you can see why it's so important we get to her as soon as possible?"

He sighs, his eyes floating between her beautiful green eyes and her luscious round tits.

Painful, too, I think. His death will be slow and painful.

"Well, Lisa," the slimy serpentapillar says as he rubs little circles on the top of her hand with his finger. "I am pleased to be able to give you some consolation. Each of our Tariluxe 2000 passenger models is equipped with a state-of-the-art med kit that includes lung expanders and permatemp blood cleansers."

Lisa scowls, flicking his hand off hers and snarling with frustration. Then, she turns to me, clears her throat, and nods. "Go ahead, Eff. Rip his fucking balls—"

She's interrupted by a high-pitch scream when I reach out and grab the little grub around his neck and pull him head-first across the counter. I try to stand him up in front of me, but his legs are limp as noodles, and he keeps dropping to the floor. I end up having to hold him up.

"Undo his pants," I tell my sweet Amazon.

She gives me a surprised look, and I'm afraid for a moment that she may not do it. Then, to my relief, she shrugs and reaches out to unbutton the bastard's pants.

"No! No, please!"

Lisa finishes popping the buttons and moves on to the zip-per without being told. Such a good girl.

"The passenger list." I growl at him once Lisa has his pants loosened.

"I can't! I'll lose my job! I'll go to jail! I can't! I just can't!" he blubbers.

I nod at Lisa to continue, and she doesn't hesitate this time. With one quick flick of her wrists, his pants are resting around his ankles.

"Shorts, too," I tell her as I reach into my pocket and re-trieve my laserblade. There's a slight hum as I flick it open.

Never wavering, my female stares at him with her steely green eyes and places her fingers into the waistband of his boxers. Fuck, my dick's getting hard as I watch her grin and slowly inch them down. My baby's heartless.

"Okay! Okay! I'll do it. I'll get it," Pat shrieks.

Lisa looks to me for direction, and I nod at her to release him. Damn if she doesn't look almost disappointed as she steps back away from the trembling coward. I give him a little shove toward his desk, trying to get my mind back on busi-ness and off my sexy little Amazon. Lachlin and Emily can't afford to have me distracted right now.

The shuttle agent leans against his desk, using it to hold himself up while he yanks his trousers back over his hips and works to fasten them with nervous fingers. Once he's buttoned, zipped and fastened, I narrow my eyes at him and make a show of flicking the laserblade closed.

"Next time, I won't stop, *Pat*. Now get me the passenger list and the last known coordinates for the shuttle, or I'm going to start removing body parts, beginning with your right nut."

Ten minutes later, both lists are in my pocket as we step out of the Taroyal Cruiselines Business Complex and onto the dark sleeping streets of downtown. My arm around Lisa, I tuck her close to my side as we duck down a narrow alley heading for my transport. My other hand rests on the molecular disbander tucked discreetly into my waistband. I'm not taking any chances with my Amazon's safety.

As I lead her through the dimly lit passage, my eyes perform a perfunctory sweep of the surrounding shops, checking for the slightest hint of danger. It's habit. In my line of work, one tends to make a lot of enemies. I've been doing this job for a while now, and my enemies are stacking up. I made a mistake once. Trusted someone I shouldn't have and forgot that I was mortal. The only reason I'm still alive today is Lachlin MacTavish.

I won't make another mistake like that one. I may look like a big, stupid oaf, but my body is a finely sculpted weapon that deals death with agility and graceful precision. I live hard, I fuck hard, and I fight hard. And I know people, know their natures. No one will ever catch me off my guard or take me by surprise again. No one.

"My gawd, Eff, you were so fucking hot back there," Lisa suddenly blurts.

Her words hit me like shots from a laser-cannon. I stagger,

trip over my feet, and stumble over an alley-flisker before diving headlong into a recycling bin.

CHAPTER TWELVE

Lisa

Dammit. I cannot believe I said that out loud. What is wrong with me?

I run across the alley to help Eff, reliving the nightmare over and over in my head. I freaked him out with my sudden outburst, scared him half to death, and made him trip over his own feet. I can't believe he stepped on a fucking cat, or something that resembled a cat if a cat were to mate with a miniature shetland pony and a potbellied pig and then have a baby. I have to give Eff props, though. He did a perfect swan dive into that garbage can.

I probably killed him. Or he killed the fucking cat. I've never heard an animal scream like that before, unless you count Eff when he flew through the air and hit that trash can. Fuck. I bet he's got a concussion at least, and it's all my fault.

I drop to my knees beside him as he drags himself out from under the garbage can.

"Oh, shit, baby. You're bleeding."

There's a wide-open gash on his forehead seeping big drops of blood that ooze down his handsome blue face. Gah! I have nothing on me to staunch the bleeding with, either. Without even thinking, I rip my shirt over my head and press it to the wound while he grumbles a weak protest.

"Just a minute. Give it a chance to stop bleeding first." I use my most authoritative voice, ignoring his complaints as I kneel beside him with my shirt pressed against his head.

"Where else are you hurt?"

"I'm okay," he tries to assure me. "I've injured nothing that won't mend quickly."

That means something else hurts, and he just doesn't want to tell me. He can feel the guilt wafting off me in spades. Now, I feel even worse.

"I'm so sorry, Eff. I didn't mean to make you fall."

"Lisa, you didn't—"

I don't let him finish. I crawl onto his lap, wrap my arms around his big blue head, and pull his face tight against me. Then, sliding my fingers into his long, black mane, I press about a thousand kisses to the top of his head.

"I'm–*smack*–so—*smack*–sorry–*smack*."

He probably thinks I'm a lunatic, a slutty lunatic. Why did I have to go and shoot my mouth off like an idiot? Why?

Because I'm horny. Let's face it, that's the honest truth. It's been so long since I've had sex, I'm not sure I even remember how to do it properly. Hell, my hymen's probably grown back by now. If I were a superhero, I'd be called the Revirginator.

All I know is this slow burn has been building with Eff for weeks now, simmering right beneath the surface of my skin, and he won't make a move. Or every time I think he's about to, something or someone interrupts us. So tonight, watching him get all muscly and aggressive back there in the Taroyal Cruiselines office had me so hot and bothered, I was afraid I might set off a smoke alarm. That bubbling pot finally blew. Dammit, I need to get laid!

"Mmph ant reath."

Huh? I lean back, still holding Eff's head in my hands, and pluck his nose out from between my boobs. His fingers clench against my waist as he sucks in a couple of big deep breaths like he's hyperventilating. Oh, crap. Or suffocating. Fuck, I almost killed him again.

"Lisa," he rumbles, his voice so low, so evocative, I can feel it resonate in my nipples.

He leans forward, growling like a bear and flashing his long, sharp canines. His eyes are dark and menacing, the quills on his arms vibrating and swaying as he licks his lips hungrily.

Holy mackerel! He's turning into a fucking animal right in front of me. When he tucks in his chin, his hazy, heated eyes burning into mine, I know I'm in trouble.

"Eff?" Shit, I broke him.

Suddenly, the alley tips on its side, and it's my turn to fly through the air screaming. I clench my eyes shut as the world around me spins out of control.

"Look at me, Amazon," Eff commands.

I crack open my eyes, surprised to find that I'm pinned to the exterior wall of a building. Caged in Eff's arms, I can't move, can barely breathe. My pulse skyrockets as I take him in. His normally sky blue eyes are almost completely black now, his nostrils flare, and his chest heaves in and out.

"Eff?" I've never seen him like this. He's always so quiet and calm, so in control. Fuck, he's like hot to the sixth power right now.

He leans into me, his nose riffling through my hair as he breathes me in. Then, he reaches down, places his finger beneath my bra strap, and whispers in my ear.

"If you don't want me, you need to tell me now."

I can't even comprehend what he's saying. My brain goes offline for a moment to reboot. When it comes back up, I nod furiously, unable to even think in full, grammatically correct sentences. My heart pounds against my ribcage while fragments of thoughts race through my mind, things like 'Eff good,' 'Lisa horny,' 'Eff fuck Lisa.'

"Tell me you want me," he says, his finger flicking my strap so that it falls to rest in the crook of my arm.

No idea what he's talking about. I'm just trying to

remember to breathe. I nod vigorously and pant. Sure. Sure. Whatever.

"Say it," he tells me again as he flicks the other strap off my shoulder.

Say what? Too much talking. No fucking. Need fucking.

He glides his fingers across my chest, winding them down over the cups of my bra and tugging. My breasts spill free, and he freezes, a low growl emanating from his throat. It's like a mating call, driving me out of my damn mind.

"Eff," I moan, my fingers finding their way into his hair and dragging him to me.

"Lisa," he groans, his hands sliding down to my waist, holding me in place as he tips his head to my breast, takes my nipple into his hot, moist mouth, and sucks. His tongue laves back and forth, round and round in big lazy circles, licking, nipping, and eviscerating me. Then, he moves to the other one.

God! It's good. Really good. Too good. But I need more. I need him in me right now, or I might actually die.

"Eff," I whine. "Please."

He squeezes my hip bones so tight, I can already feel the bruises forming.

"Say it, Lis. Tell me what you want," he demands.

Then, he presses my nipple between his sharp front teeth and bites me, hard and punishing.

"You!" I yip. "Fuck, I want you, Eff."

Talk being cheap, and Eff being super frugal with words, anyway, he doesn't say anything more. He slams his lips into mine, robbing me of any coherent thoughts I may have had left as he thrusts his tongue into my mouth. Firm lips take control of the kiss, and I fucking love it, revel in it, giving myself over to the possessiveness of it. It is hungry and wet, forceful and all-consuming. Epherus Zinto owns me.

"Got to . . ." he groans, yanking me around and pressing

me roughly into the wall. He jerks my hips toward him and wrenches my pants down with one hand. " . . . be in you."

I'm like a fucking cat on a scratching post, mewling and whimpering with my head down and hands planted firmly on the wall. Finally! I'm so ready for this, so ready for him. Standing on my tiptoes, I bend over as far as I can and rest my cheek against the wall while I wiggle my ass shamelessly at him. Oh, yeah, I am. I'm ready.

I hear the sound of a zipper, pants sliding against skin, and then coins spilling out into the alleyway. My pulse ratchets up another notch, and if I push my ass out any further, it'll be in a different zip code than the rest of my body. 'Hurry' is all I can think as my pussy clenches with excitement, eager for my blue assassin. Then, his big, calloused hand presses into my back, right between my shoulder blades.

"Don't. Fucking. Move," he rumbles, and it sounds both commanding and pleading at the same time.

Move? Is he serious? At this point, a Goridian warship could land in the middle of the square playing the Tarilean national anthem as the President of the USA walks out holding hands with my third grade teacher, Sister Penny, and they'd still have to wait for us to finish.

"I'm releasing my cock," he tells me.

Uh . . . Did he just say he was 'releasing his cock'? As in 'releasing the hounds' or a 'big can of whoop ass' or something? I almost chuckle except I'm too excited to see what his cock does once it's free.

His hand pushes harder into my back, pressing me against the wall so hard, I can't move. He grasps my hip tightly with the other, his fingers gripping my hipbone firmly as he places sweet kisses on my lower back. Oh, yeah. Yes. Yes. That feels good. I nearly orgasm when long, thick fingers begin slicking through my sopping folds, dragging moans of ecstasy from my lungs. My toes curl, and my nipples ache as he dips a digit inside me.

Uh . . . hold the phone. My eyes fly open, and I gasp, suddenly realizing that he has one hand on my back and one on my hip, his fingers wrapped around my hip bone and squeezing so hard, I'll probably have bruises tomorrow. So unless he has a third hand somewhere I haven't seen yet . . . whose fingers are those down there?

I cry out suddenly, and all logic dissipates like a puff of smoke in a windstorm as another digit is added to the mix down there, then another, and another. Until finally, they're all over the place, drilling and wiggling inside me, sliding up and down my slick lips, wrapping around my clit, and . . . fuck, yes! Sucking on it like a vacuum cleaner.

"Can't be gentle. So wet. So beautiful. Fucking love it, love you, my Amazon," he babbles, practically speaking in tongues as the assault on my pussy continues.

"Eff," I pant, not even faking the tears in my eyes this time. This has to be the sweetest fucking torture I've ever suffered.

I nearly start sobbing when the tendrils begin to retreat. But then, they gently part my lips, and his massive cock spears into me. It's like a damn anaconda, alive and snaking in and out of me, expanding and writhing, wriggling into spots no one has ever reached before. It hurts and feels wonderful, hard and flexible at the same time. And he's still not fully inside me.

Two large, powerful hands bear down on my shoulders, and all those fingers downstairs begin gently caressing my thighs, my clit, my ass.

So he's got dick tentacles, and his cock is apparently a live snake. Who fucking cares? It feels incredible. Oh, hell yes. There's no going back after this.

I squeak as he nudges a little further inside me, then try to relax the feminine muscles that are currently intent on keeping him out. For the first time ever, I seem to be at odds with my pussy.

"Okay?" he asks, his voice strained and gravelly.

"Yes," I pant impatiently, secretly afraid he might give up. "Keep going. Don't stop."

He grunts and flexes. "Gods. You're so fucking tight, Amazon."

Yes, yes. I'm the Revirginatrix. Less talking, more fucking. I wiggle my hips, working a little more of him inside, and apparently poking the sleeping Aurelian bear. He hauls back his hips and drives into me like a man possessed, like an alien possessing a female. Then, with one last mighty thrust, he's fully sheathed.

He yells, I yodel, somewhere nearby, that fucking cat screams, and while I'm so full I can feel the tip of his dick tickling my tonsils, I can't help but squirm and writhe against him. He stays there for a moment, his hot breath puffing against my ear as he rocks into me. His fingers tweak and pinch my nipples while his tentacle softly strokes my clit, and I'm already nearing the finish line. But then, he angles his hips and bumps against my ass a little harder, nearly lifting my toes off the ground each time. I've never felt anything so good in my life. At least, not until his tentacle latches on while he plows back into me with the force of a Tarilean space shuttle. And when a second tentacle breaches my back hole, it's game over.

"Epherus!" I scream at the top of my lungs as my entire body explodes in climax.

That's what we call taking the fucking Oscar back home. I give it up to him, surrender the Big O, soak his cock, suffer la petite mort. Whatever you want to call it, I either have it or I give it to him. Thank fuck he's holding me up, or I'd be a dark gooey spot on the pavement.

"Fuck!" Eff shouts abruptly, and a booming clap of thunder explodes in the alley, right before my ass catches fire.

I scream, my butt blazing as he ruts against me like a madman fighting for the last hit of Clozapine. With a grizzly roar, he drives into me one last time, and I feel the crack of more thunder strike against my other cheek. He grunts with several quick thrusts as he jerks and twitches inside me. And I'm off to the races again, melting for the second time on his beautiful, gushing cock.

We stand like that for a minute afterward, Eff pressed into me, me pressed into the wall as we try to catch our breaths. He feels so damn good, I'm not sure if that cat's back or if my pussy is purring. Either way, it's heaven with his broad chest blanketing my back, his strong arms locked around my stomach, and his warm seed spilling down my thighs.

Oh, shit! Wait a minute. Warm seed spilling down my thighs?

CHAPTER THIRTEEN

Lachlin

"Her name is Aliyah." I almost whisper, afraid saying it too loud might somehow conjure her. "She's the eldest daughter of the Iwoehon Emperor, Kwanlo Azandar, and the next in line for the throne. Weirdly enough, the emperor has no sons, only daughters. Seventeen and counting, most of them by different women in his harem.

"Although, I suppose he could have sons by now. More than half of the women were pregnant when I left, all the younger ones. He collects them the way some men collect wallets. Most of the concubines are from planets they raid or occupy, but some are Iowehonians. None of them are there willingly, though. To Iwoehonians, the larger the harem, the more powerful one is presumed to be.

"Technically, Aliyah is not a princess, even though everyone considers her to be one. Her mother is the emperor's chief consort, but she is not his queen. Aliyah is the only child between the two of them, and he has no legitimate heirs. Yet. I think because of that, she's also the favorite of all the royal children and the only female in Iwoehon permitted to keep her own harem. For the most part, the society is pretty misogynistic."

"There were others besides you?" Duchess asks, her voice soft and hesitant.

I sigh, guilt suddenly weighing very heavy on my heart. "Yes. Many others."

Giving my head a shake, I put them out of my mind. At least for now so I can get through my story.

"The Iwoehon Galaxy itself is huge and lies at the very edge of the Milky Way. It's home to the cruelest, vilest and most black-hearted pirates in the universe. They survive solely by their swords, feeding on the fear and degradation of their enemies, and even their subordinates in a lot of cases. They have no compassion, no mercy, and no humanity. Princess Aliyah is no exception. In truth, she may even be worse than most."

I pause, reflecting on the darkest period of my life. I haven't allowed myself to do that since my escape. It would be too easy to slip back into that hopeless black depression and too hard to climb back out again.

"I'd been at the pub the night I was taken, which was nothing unusual after Mum died. It was just so hard to be around Aine and Pop. There were too many memories, too much pain. So I drank, a lot. Looking back, I regret that more than anything. They needed me, and I wasn't there for them, even before I was taken."

That's the first time I've said it aloud, and fuck, it feels good to finally get it off my chest. I sucked as a brother and a son. I let my family down, and I need absolution like I need my next breath.

"Anyway, I was walking home the first time they captured me. I was stumbling across an empty field and probably not even a hundred yards from our house."

"The first time?"

I hear the surprise in Duchess' voice.

"Yeah. I escaped three times and was recaptured twice before I finally got away." Three miserable, fucked-up times that nearly broke me.

"But I'm getting ahead of myself. That first night, I was so drunk, I didn't even fight them. When I finally sobered up, I was onboard the Dracarus, naked and cuffed spread-eagle to Aliyah's bed. She almost seemed normal at first. We . . . uh . . . She used me, used my body, several times that night, and I didn't even try to stop her. I was still really confused, had no idea what was going on. I even thought it was some chick's hot fantasy I was helping her play out." I frown, my head moving from side to side as if to reject that thought altogether.

"She was beautiful?" my Duchess asks, her voice small and trembling as her fingers twist nervously in her lap.

Not sure why, but I think about lying. I don't, though. Sighing, I nod.

"She was beautiful. At least, at first, I thought she was. It didn't take long to realize, though, that it wasn't a fantasy at all. It was more like a nightmare. And Aliyah was a fucking monster.

"It went on like that for a while. I don't know how long because I wasn't allowed to leave our quarters or have access to electronics of any kind. I just sat there in that empty room and stared at the four walls most days, not even a window to look out of. Looking back, I think it was her way of making me desperate for company, for companionship. So that I'd be happy, even grateful to see her when she finally did show up.

"When she was away, they kept me locked in, always alone. Visitors were prohibited. Clothes, too. I wasn't allowed to dress unless it was, well, something she wanted to see me in. Meals were delivered through a gen-ex dispenser, and I had an adjoining lavatory for showers and whatever.

"Every night when she'd return, they would hit me with some kind of electromagnetic charge that would have me jerking around in agony on the floor. I'd lose control of my body every time. Once, I even pissed myself. Her guards would come in, pick me up, and cuff me to the bed before it wore off. Then, they'd leave, she'd come in, and it would start all over again.

"I begged her to release me, just drop me off somewhere on a deserted planet, a war planet, anything. I didn't care. I just wanted out of there. She never would, of course. I even tried to reject her advances, but that never worked, either. My goddam body betrayed me every night. She made sure of that. I was so fucking weak. She'd laugh at me, laugh at my pathetic attempts to resist like I was useless, ridiculous. And no matter how much I threatened or begged, she wouldn't stop, wouldn't tell me anything except that I belonged to her and that I was the property of the Iwoehon crown. She said the sooner I accepted it, the easier it would be on everyone, especially me."

I take a deep breath, not sure if I can get through this next part without breaking. But I need to. I need to get it out.

"I'd never felt lower in my life, never felt so fucking worthless. I worried about Aine and Pop constantly. Were they okay? Was there enough money coming in without me for them to eat and pay the bills? Did they think I was dead? Hell, they were still reeling from Nana's and Mum's deaths. Then to lose me, too? I couldn't imagine what they were going through. Or maybe I could, and that's what made it so bad? Ant it was bad, Duchess. Really bad, but then, it got even worse.

"For whatever reason, Aliyah was absurdly fond of me, treated me like a favorite toy, even decided to make me her chief consort, whatever the fuck that meant. But after a while, it wasn't enough for her to know that I was there, existing solely for her pleasure, to satisfy her every whim. None of it mattered if no one else saw it, if they didn't know. So, she started bringing people with her to watch, mainly her sisters, to start. Always high-ranking women of the royal court. Always an audience.

"At first, she would only let them look, never touch. She was insanely jealous, especially of her sisters. She'd make them stand around the bed and watch while she got me ready, rubbing oils all over me, licking my cock and massaging my balls with lotion. I tried so hard, so fucking hard to ignore it, ignore her and make my dick stay soft. It just . . . well. I couldn't do it. She always got her way, got her penetration one way or another while the others looked on or took care of themselves.

"As it went on, though, eventually, even that wasn't enough, either. She started bringing men along with the women, and they'd spend entire nights smoking opiata, drinking kocho, and fucking. And soon after that, I made it on to the menu, too."

I swallow, trying to force the bile back down my throat, wondering what Duchess is thinking. She's probably sick, too. Fuck, I wouldn't blame her. Will she ever want to touch me again? I take a deep breath and try to decide how I want to finish the story.

"I'd already tried to escape twice and was facing death if I got caught again when I learned about the Aurelian assassin captured by the emperor's elite warriors. One night when they were all wasted on morphaline, I overheard Aliyah talking to Lishaf, one of the emperor's cabinet members. She said she wanted him. She wanted that assassin and was totally pissed that her father was about to execute such a 'succulent male specimen.'

"I really didn't give it too much thought other than feeling sorry for the guy, whoever he was, and disappointed that his mission hadn't been successful, especially if he was there to kill her. But somehow, Aliyah was able to get to him, to have him dragged to our room, *her* room. I've always assumed she either bribed or blackmailed Lishaf into breaking him out of his cell. Her guards, of course, were loyal to her, but none of them had access to the emperor's prisons. I guess I'll never know how she pulled that off."

I frown and shrug, lost in thought as I recall my first glimpse of Epherus Zinto. He was beaten, bruised and bloody, his body still twitching from the electroshock as two guards dragged him into the room, one on each side, straining beneath his enormous weight.

"Anyway, it must have been a crime of opportunity because she wasn't expecting him right then. She was actually surprised when they showed up. He was still mostly under the electroshock, but it was starting to wear off. They got panicked. Apparently, they didn't expect the big ox to come out it so fast. They didn't even have time to shock me before they had to drag him inside.

"Eff was pissed and growling and somehow managed to get to his feet. He started stumbling around, swinging at everything and everyone, including Aliyah. He managed to land a good hit on one of the guards who was trying to secure me, and that was all the opening I needed.

"Long story short, I wrestled a blaster from one of the guards, killed two of them, and escaped with Eff. We fought our way to his ship, killed every guard who got in our way, and got the fuck out of dodge."

"What happened to Aliyah?"

"She ran after I shot the first guard in her room. Smart girl. She would have been the next one to die. The last time I saw her, she was standing by the transports with what was left of her guard detail, screaming for them to kill me."

"Kill you? But, I thought . . . I thought she loved you?"

"Hm. Loved me," I repeat, scoffing as I stir my feet around in the crystal clear water. "Iwoehonians don't know love, Duchess. They know murder, rape, slavery, how to inflict their will upon others." I tug my shirt over my head and twist around to present her my back, to show her just how much Aliyah *loved* me. "She had this done after my first escape attempt."

I can't see it, but I know all too well what my back looks like, covered with scars from the whippings and the shiny puckered skin across my right shoulder blade where she branded two lazy S's. Beneath it are the words 'property of the Iwoehon throne'.

I flinch as Duchess' fingertips skim over the cursed mark. Closing my eyes, I focus on her feather-light touch, so warm and soothing. Then, my heart nearly implodes when I feel the gentle press of her lips against the marred, deformed skin on my back.

"Duchess," I whisper.

When I turn to her, she dips her head, sniffles, then raises her sparkling tear-filled eyes to mine.

"Lachlin MacTavish, you are not weak. You're one of the strongest men I've ever met. I've never felt so safe, so protected with anyone as I do when I'm with you. You're smart and kind and beautiful."

I watch as a single tear escapes down her rosy cheek.

"And, *I* love you."

CHAPTER FOURTEEN

Emily

I can't believe I just blurted that out, but it's true. I said it, and I don't regret it. I try my best to keep my tears in check, but a few manage to get through as he stares at me in stunned silence. Or maybe it's disbelief. Maybe he can't believe I said it, either?

If I could just stop shaking. I'm not sure if it's nerves, anger or just too much emotion, but I feel like I'm crawling out of my skin. What I do know is that I feel sorry for that Iwoehonian bitch if I ever get my hands on her. I'll kill her. I'll wrap my hands around her slutty neck and strangle her to death.

God, I wish he'd say something. If he laughs or acts disgusted by what I said, I can always laugh it off and say I meant love like a sisterly kind of thing. A sick sister who wants to strip off his clothes and lick him from head to toe and —

"Come here," he whispers, leaning toward me as his gaze drops to my lips.

He's going to kiss me. Fuck, he's going to kiss me. My heart is thumping louder than a cheap whore's bed, my pulse racing as my tongue snakes out to wet my lips. I tilt my head and close my eyes, giddy with anticipation. And then, he does it.

Soft lips press against mine, once, twice, and again. His lips part, and his tongue begins lapping lightly at the seam of my mouth until I open and let him in. And then, I'm kissing him back. I'm kissing Lachlin MacTavish.

His tongue is firm and thorough in its exploration, leaving nothing untouched or unaffected. I'm affected, all right. My whole body is affected. My hand reaches out to touch his face, but it's not enough. I slide my fingers into his hair, fisting and tugging as he pulls me closer. A shiver rolls through me as the world around us fades away, replaced with tongues and lips and hands and panting breaths.

He tastes so good. He tastes like Lachlin, an unforgettable mixture of male, sex and perfectly aged whisky, strong whisky that's gone straight to my head. I feel drunk just from a kiss, his kiss, like nothing I've ever experienced. I've never been kissed like this before, and I doubt I ever will be again.

"Lachlin," I whisper into his mouth.

"Duchess," he growls, grabbing the hem of my dress and peeling it over my head until I'm sitting in nothing but my bra. Then, nothing at all as it lands on top of my dress.

He leans back, his hands holding mine as his half-lidded eyes roll over my body.

"Fuck, Duchess. You're perfect."

"So are you," I reply honestly.

"Right." He smirks, as if I'm lying.

I'm about to tell him it's true, possibly even say something as dorky as he's the most perfect man I've ever seen, when he pops up, rips off his pants, and plunges headfirst into the water. Just dives in without another word.

I sit there stupefied for a moment, my big maw gaping until Lachlin reappears in front of me several seconds later spraying and spluttering and laughing. He reaches his hand out of the water and scrapes it over his face, smoothing back his hair and smiling like a naughty skinny-dipper.

"You just mooned me," I inform him.

"I figured turn-about was fair play." He chuckles. "Come swim with me."

Uh . . . this is really not where I expected that hot, steamy kiss to lead. But what the hell? I'm already naked.

"Okay." I laugh, jumping off the bank and splashing right into his waiting arms, arms that I knew would catch me. And they did.

Now, he wraps them around me and pulls me tight against him. Face-to-face, I breathe in his warm breath, then my tongue peeks out to taste his inviting lips. I kiss him. Or maybe he kisses me. Either way, we kiss, and it's not the soft, gentle kiss from before. This one is hard and passionate, hot and urgent. This kiss feels like possession. My arms loop around his neck, my fingers plunge into the thick wet strands of his hair, and once again, I lose myself in all things Lachlin MacTavish.

He holds me so tight, I can barely breathe, my toes scraping the bottom of the pool. And when his hands glide across my back and come to rest on my naked ass, I shudder while goosebumps swim up and down my arms. Wrapping my legs around his waist, I taste the little niche between his shoulder and his neck as he grinds his cock against me.

I haven't had a man since Earth was a little blue dot in my rearview mirror. Needless to say, things escalate pretty quickly. Never much for water sports, I'm happy when he starts traipsing through the water toward the shallow end of the pool, me clinging to him like a starfish the entire way.

He places me gently on the bank, grabbing hold of my ankles and pressing me into the grass as he implements a move that would make a pro wrestler proud. I blink, and suddenly, my knees are bent up to my neck and my legs splayed out like a turkey at Thanksgiving. When he leans forward and nuzzles my pussy, a shower of sparks shoots through my whole body.

"Fuck," he murmurs. "Look at that beautiful pink pussy."

"Lachlin," I moan, his dirty talk alone almost enough to send me spiraling over the edge.

My hands grasp at the ground, at the grass, at my hair,

trying feverishly to find something natural to occupy themselves. It's not like I can wrap them in the bed covers, and I'm not much of an exhibitionist, so playing with my own nipples is out. I mean, I don't want to wash dishes or whittle a St. Bernard or anything. I want to touch Lachlin, maybe pull his hair, claw his back, jerk his dick, anything, but I can't reach him.

"Do you feel it, Duchess? Tell me you feel it."

Fuck, yeah, I feel it, I almost say, but think maybe that's not what he means.

"What?" I pant. "Feel what?"

"The water," he says. "The pool, her healing powers."

"Um." Hell, I have no idea what I feel. I'm naked on a bank with Lachlin MacTavish's face between my legs. I don't feel anything right now except so turned on I think I might combust any second and burn the whole fucking jungle down. I could instigate a small natural disaster if we're not careful.

Then, I feel his warm, firm tongue slicing through my sensitive folds in one long, mind-blowing lick that ends with my clit sucked between his teeth. I scream so loud that any search parties within a twenty-five mile radius should be here to pick us up within the hour. And thank goodness I finally have somewhere to put my hands. My nails dig into his scalp, my fingers twist in his hair, and I wriggle and whine, riding his face like a fucking pro. Then, he adds a finger to the mix, and just like the rodeo cowgirls, I make it for about eight seconds before I break.

"Lachlin!" I scream at the top of my lungs, ensuring that any of the search parties who may have missed it the first time get a second chance to lock onto our position.

I come so hard, I see cupcakes on the backs of my eyelids, which actually surprises me. I don't normally see food when I climax. Maybe it's because I'm hungry, I don't know. The rest of it is normal enough. I gasp, cry, warble and speak in foreign languages as Lachlin laps at me, groaning as he carries me through a championship climax. My pussy clenches around his finger over and over like it's trying to swallow him whole. I needed this. Heck yeah, I needed this.

Still in the grip of ecstasy, I blink my eyes open to find his face hovering directly above me, his body aligned with mine. I never even heard him get out of the water. He's like some kind of oral sex ninja.

He falls on me, his lips crashing into mine, his hands squeezing my breasts and pinching my nipples until I actually cry out. My hips buck at the air as his tongue blazes a fiery trail to my breasts, and suddenly, I'm engulfed in Lachlin. He's everywhere, all over me—sucking, licking, biting, squeezing, stroking. I'm at the tipping point, but still, I need more.

"Can't wait," he growls, his fingers splayed wide around my inner thighs, spreading me even further as the tip of his cock slides up and down through my slick folds.

"Yes," I pant because I can't think of any words more than two-syllables long right now.

"Emily," he whispers as the fat head of his huge cock nudges open my still throbbing channel.

Finally, he enters me. Just a little bit, just enough to freeze my lungs and keep a groan wedged into the back of my throat. It's not enough and too much at the same time.

"Lachlin, please," I whimper as his fingers press into the tender flesh of my thighs.

That's all the incentive he needs to complete the job, slamming into me so hard, I hear the bells of Notre Dame ringing in my ears.

"Ah, fuck! Son-of-a-bitch."

I barely recognize the words as he grinds them out between clenched teeth. Hell, I barely recognize where I'm at right now, and then, he really gets down to business.

All I can do is grit my teeth and hang on. It's like riding a washing machine down a gravel road full of potholes. I've never been fucked like this before, desperate and explosive. Violent. He groans when I sink my teeth into his shoulder, and I nearly convulse after he slaps me hard on the ass.

This is round two for me, and already, I'm working at beating my best time. My eyes closed, ululating like a gypsy herding sheep, I'm almost there when Lachlin pounds into me like a sledgehammer one last time and gives me a punishing smack on my other butt cheek.

"Goddamit! Duchess!"

He throws his head back and shouts, scaring the absolute shit out of me for a minute. I still come like a freight train, but it really did scare me.

I peep open an eye to make sure no wild beasts have wandered into the grotto or that damn monkey wasn't lured back by all the phenomenal sex going on, but all I see is Lachlin's beautiful face. And he does look beautiful releasing into me, head thrown back with jaws clenching, the ropy cords in his neck thick and bulging and the muscles in his arms flexed and extended.

"Fuck. Me." He groans, and I finally realize what's going on. Lachlin MacTavish is an angry fucker.

I don't mean he's angry as in cross or annoyed. He just fucks that way, like a madman. I'm not complaining, believe me. I happen to like angry fucking. I adore angry fucking. It's my favorite kind of fucking as of five minutes ago. I wonder if he swears every time he comes? I'm determined to find out.

"Duchess," he puffs in my ear, easing his weight on top of me as he plants kisses down my neck. "You feel so good, babe."

And he's a post-coital sweet talker, too. I've hit the "fucking" jackpot!

We spend the next few minutes catching our breaths, whispering and giggling. Actually, I giggle. Lachlin chuckles, and

I think he really lets loose with a guffaw once or twice when we were talking about Lisa and Eff. It's wonderful, almost as good as the sex itself. Almost. And if I hadn't already known that I was in love with Lachlin MacTavish, I'd know it now for sure.

He rolls over, props his head on his elbow, and smiles at me. "Thank you."

"You're welcome," I giggle. Then, I notice he's not kidding around anymore, and I get serious pretty damn quick, too. "For what, Lachlin?"

He stares at me for several seconds, his lips curving to hint at a smile and his eyes shining with so many feelings, I can't even pin one of them down.

"For healing me," he says.

My heart squeezes in my chest, and I struggle to swallow back the sudden onset of tears. Shaking my head, I reach out to caress his face and shift the mood back into the light.

"It wasn't me. It was Urgowa."

He shakes his head. "No, it was all you, baby."

CHAPTER FIFTEEN

Lachlin

She's so beautiful, it almost hurts to look at her. It's not just skin deep, either. Not with Duchess. She's beautiful on the inside, too, and warm and kind and funny. I don't know how I could have ever thought her a cold fish. That idea is almost laughable now. I haven't felt this good, this happy just to be alive in years. In the last twenty-four hours, we've been shot at, shipwrecked, concussed, attacked by wild animals, and nearly killed by a damn mountain. That's not even considering that we're stranded in the middle of a hostile jungle where everything wants to eat us or fuck us up. So why the hell am I so happy?

She said she loved me. Did she mean it the way I hope she meant it? Or did she mean she loves me like a friend? A good friend who she fucks. I almost said it back. It was right on the tip of my tongue. But I didn't. I won't, not until I'm absolutely sure how she feels.

"Are you hungry? Want to get something to eat?"

She looks at me like I've just grown two heads, and I almost chuckle.

"Yes, I'm starving, actually. Why? You don't happen to have a couple of extra cheeseburgers on you, do you?"

"No cheeseburgers, but I bet we can find something to tide us over." I stand up and brush at all the dirt stuck to me as I walk over and scoop up my pants.

"Count me in. We didn't have any dinner last night, and

all I had for lunch yesterday was a salad. Or that red stuff that passes as a salad here."

"I think I saw some berries over there we can eat." I step into my pants and nod at a fluffy blue bush with scads of big pink berries dripping off it. "Those are flickerberries. Believe it or not, they taste like chicken."

"Everything tastes like chicken." She laughs. Then, she stands up, her magnificent body bathed in moonlight as she swipes at the grass stuck to her legs. "I need to rinse off first."

And she's smart, too. I forgot to list that one in the assets column. If I'd been half as smart, I would have rinsed my legs off before I put my pants back on. Then, they wouldn't feel like they're wrapped in sandpaper right now.

"You know," I call out to her as I tug my shirt over my head. "I'm pretty sure those bushes over there on the other side are corkenberries. I've had them before. They're really good."

"Oh, I love corkenberries! Shauna made us a —" She stops mid-sentence, standing up to her thighs in the water and gasping so loud, my heart skips two beats.

"Duchess!" I leap over a boulder and stub my toe on a rock trying to get to her, prepared to dive in and wrestle a fucking sabertooth tiger shark. But I don't see anything. "What?"

She turns to look at me, her eyes round and full of panic. "Nothing. Sorry. I didn't mean to scare you."

"It's obviously not nothing, Duchess. Tell me. What's wrong?"

"I . . . We . . ." She looks down at the water for a moment, then back at me. "Lachlin, I'm not on any birth control."

My heart sighs and settles, my muscles relax, and I release the breath I didn't even realize I was holding. Thank God there's nothing wrong. Wait. She's not on birth control. We just had sex. Without protection. She could be pregnant right now. With my child. I cock my head and wait for the panic to kick in. Any second now, I'm going to freak the fuck out, be overwhelmed with turmoil, and run around in circles hyperventilating. Any second.

Several seconds pass as we stare at each other, and still nothing.

"Lachlin," she says.

"Yeah?"

"Did you hear me? Did you hear what I said?" She shakes her head at me. "I'm not on birth control. We didn't use any protection."

"I heard you." I smile. "It'll be okay. Wash up and let's eat."

She crinkles her nose and narrows her eyes at me. I never noticed before, but she gets the cutest little dimple on her forehead, right at the bridge of her nose, when she frowns. Chuckling, I turn around and head back toward the berry bushes.

I've managed to pick nearly half the flickerberries and piled them into my shirt when Duchess saunters over.

"You okay?" I ask her, not that I have a plan to handle things if she says no.

"Yeah. I guess," she says, still looking a little shell-shocked.

"It'll be fine. You'll see. And chances are so slim—"

"Right. Let's not jinx it, okay? Don't say it. Now, how can I help?"

I grin and shake my head. "You want to go over there and pick some of the corkenberries?"

"Sure. Point me at them." Her gaze darts all around the grotto like they're eager for a distraction.

"Over there." I point across the pool to a shrub with red, banana-shaped berries hanging from the branches.

"Cool." She trots off, and I return to picking flickerberries. "Hey! What about these?"

I look up in time to see her pluck a purple, softball-sized nut off a low tree branch.

"No. Throw that away. Those are hooky nuts, and they'll

make you really sick."

She chunks it like a live grenade into the forest and cringes as though she half expects it explode when it lands. I guess I can't blame her. We've had enough shit luck this trip. We don't need to tempt fate.

"These are good, though." I reach over and tug on a vine that's covered with giant orange blooms and hold it up for her to see. "These are hestersuckle blossoms. They're a little sweet, but they're filling."

"Oh, there's lots of those around here," she says, pointing all around the grotto. "I can pick those."

Duchess returns a short time later with her arms full of blossoms and berries. I lead her over to a small carpet of plush blue grass beside the falls where I've placed the rest of the food. I've even managed to find what I think are wild pizzlenuts. At least, I'm about ninety-five percent sure they're pizzlenuts. We'll have to decide if we're brave enough to risk them.

"Let's eat." I wave my hand toward the picnic-perfect patch of moss and grass.

"Why, thank you," she says, giggling as she sits down.

Sitting there beside the falls, we watch the suns come up in silence while we gorge on corkenberries, hestersuckle blossoms, flickerberries, and preister fruit with their fleshy brown globes that taste surprisingly like homemade bread. We even eat some of the pizzlenuts after I crack one open, confirm they look like pizzlenuts, and my confidence level goes up to ninety-nine percent. We eat until we're stuffed, then Duchess packs some of the leftover berries into our med kit with the rest of the supplies.

"Okay. What's the plan?"

She looks at me with all the trust and confidence in the world as she waits for me to reply. I have to smile when I realize how much I like it. More than that, I love it. I love the way she's looking at me, and I don't care if she's pregnant. No, more than that, even. I hope she is pregnant. She's the one. I know it like I know that north leads to the capital city of Tartopia.

"What?" She grins nervously.

"Just thinking," I reply. "We have a choice. I haven't seen any sign of wildlife here in this grotto. We can try to take a little nap and finish recharging. Or we can pack a few more of these nuts and berries, refill our water bottle, and keep going. It's up to you."

She pinches her lower lip between her fingers and taps on it. "You know, I feel fantastic, almost like I've had a full night's sleep already. In fact, I don't remember the last time I felt this good. Don't roll your eyes at me, but I think it's the water."

"Oh, I'm not rolling my eyes," I say as I stalk slowly toward her. "But maybe it isn't actually the healing pools."

Enjoying the brief look of confusion that flits across her face as she takes a hesitant step back, I keep going. "Maybe it's something else? Something else entirely."

"Uh . . ." She lifts her hands out in front of her as if that will hold me back. It doesn't. I continue advancing on her, watching her grow more and more nervous. "What are you doing?"

"Thinking about dessert," I tell her.

She laughs nervously. "You really like tempting fate, don't you?"

I shake my head, a predatory smile breaking across my face as she runs out of bank and has nowhere else to go. "You saying you think this is fate, Duchess?"

She looks behind her to confirm there's nowhere left to go, not without jumping into the water. Then, she turns back to face me. "Uh . . . I didn't say that. Exactly."

"So, you do think this is fate?" I wave my hand between the two of us, liking the sound of that more than I probably should. "The two of us? Here. Together."

Reaching out, I grab her hands and tug her to me, locking my arms around her waist. I stare down into her wide eyes and have to wonder. Are we fated to be together? Is she my destiny?

"Um . . . maybe," she whispers.

"Do you want me?" I need to know. I gotta know.

Her gaze drops to my chest, and she licks her lips in a nervous gesture. Then, almost imperceptibly, she nods.

"Say it," I tell her, placing my fingers beneath her chin and raising her face so that she looks me in the eye. "Tell me you want me."

"I want you," she whispers.

I smile so bright, not even the glowing rocks beneath the pool compare. I reach for a wayward lock of her hair and tuck it securely behind her ear.

"I want you, too," I tell her, confident that those little words sum up the whole of my feelings, not just the current state of my dick.

I'm pretty sure she gets my meaning as her lips part with a tiny gasp. Her round eyes search mine, and I can almost see her thoughts, her doubts and fears. The need for reassurance is written on her beautiful face, evident in the way her body trembles. She needs convincing? No problem.

I kiss the shit out of her, leaving her no safe quarter, nowhere to hide from me. I take it all. Everything she's got. Then, I lay her back down on the soft grass and make love to her until there's not a trace of doubt left anywhere, until I'm sure the only name she can remember is mine.

CHAPTER SIXTEEN

Lisa

Oh my God. They know. Somehow, they know we just fucked like wild monkeys. I can tell. Cora keeps throwing me these strange looks, and Maggie won't quit smirking at us. This is all Eff's fault, dammit. That smile on his face is totally inappropriate, not to mention suspicious, and he definitely needs to stop that humming beneath his breath. He hasn't even threatened to kill anybody since we got here.

Crap, maybe it's me? Maybe it's the way he keeps making me smile every time I look at him? Okay, we just need to act normal. Throw them off the scent. Oh, no, the scent. I lean over as close I dare, inhaling deeply and taking in as much of Eff's natural scent as humanly possible. It goes straight to my head, and instantly I feel warm and content, secure. Fuck, aroused again. Dam, I've got it bad.

"How about you, Lisa?"

My eyes go wide, and I realize I've missed an entire conversation. I give Cora a sheepish look. "Um . . ."

"She feels the same way I do," Eff suddenly speaks up, looking at me with laughing eyes. The dirty dog knows exactly where my mind has drifted. "We believe they're alive, and we're going to find them. You're welcome to join the search, if you like."

Thank fuck he was paying attention. I nod in agreement. Yeah, what he said.

"Horok?" Cora looks over at her husband, and it suddenly

occurs to me that's exactly how I've been gazing at Eff, too. Like the depth of my next breath, the course of my future health and happiness depends on his next few words out of his mouth. Shit. I got it bad.

Horok frowns, pushes himself away from the enormous conference table, and stands. He glances at everyone briefly before his eyes settle back on Cora. Shoving his hands into his pockets, he begins to pace contemplatively across the jam-packed meeting room.

"I believe they're alive, too. And I'm glad Eff is going to search for them, but you are not going with them, my little goddess." He turns, and his eyes settle back on Cora. "I don't have to tell you how dangerous it is out there, and in your condition, Amavi . . ."

Her condition? What condition is that? And then, it hits me. Holy shit! The room explodes into excited chatter, every-one whooping and shouting their congratulations all at once. Well, everyone except me, Shauna and Maggie. We stare at each other in disbelief.

It's not that she's pregnant that has us shocked. The way those two go at it, I'm surprised it took this long. No, what has us boggled is why she didn't tell us before now. We're not just work associates or fellow crew members. We're best friends, confidantes, and for us to find out at the same time as everyone else? Well, that's a bit hurtful. That's all I'm saying. Now is not the time to dwell on it, though. We have much more important things to deal with at the moment.

When the chatter settles down, Cora looks embarrassed, maybe even a little upset. Horok stands over her, squeezing her shoulder as he gives her an apologetic smile.

"Well, thank you, everyone. We didn't intend to just blurt it out like this." She frowns at Horok, then looks to me, Maggie and Shauna. "I'm sorry, guys. I only found out for sure yesterday. I was going to tell you last night, but it just didn't seem right without Emily."

Just that quick, all is forgiven. We smile and nod, a silent indication that we'll celebrate later, when our Emily is back home where she belongs.

"But Horok's right. I can't go."

"Of course not. We wouldn't let you go, anyway," I tell her, totally ignoring the fact that I might be in the same boat as her. Well, except that she has a husband and three babies already.

Geez. I could be pregnant right now, and all I have is a cranky assassin . . . *what*? Lover? Boyfriend? I almost snort. I shake my head, trying to clear away the cluttered thoughts. Freaking out right now is not going to help anyone.

"We've got this, Cora." I smile at her. "Actually, with the coordinates nailed down, we'll be able to move faster if we travel light. We could fly out as soon as we're done here, find them, and be back home in time for supper."

"There's no need to place our femkis in harm's way like this. Now that we have the coordinates, I'll send troops," Councilor Ja'Baal states authoritatively. "Experienced trackers and soldiers. I wouldn't be able to rest knowing that I didn't do everything possible to bring Emily, or her remains, home safely. Oh, and your brother, too, of course," he says to Aine.

"Right. Of course." Aine cocks an irritated brow at Ja'Baal, and her entire demeanor seems to shift. "Listen, Councilor, I appreciate the offer, but femki or not, I don't need your troops. I'll go find my brother myself. And may the goddess have mercy on anything that gets in my way."

Damn. Who is this girl? My eyes widen as I watch Aine posture, the quiet little waif who's always seemed so nice and sweet, the perfect daughter, the ideal wife and baby-mama. Admittedly, in the past, I've found her to be a bit soft, maybe even a little too feminine and needy to survive on her own out here. Now, for the first time, I'm seeing something I never no-ticed before—courage, strength, determination. I see a fighter.

"Whoa. Slow down there, my little warrior princess," Griz tells her. "I'm sure Lachlin and Emily are both fine. Stay here with Theo and my dam. I'll go with Eff, and we'll bring your brother home to you, I swear."

"I'm coming, too." Bruce stands and looks at everyone. "Doona you kids worry yer heads. Lachlin'll be taking good care of your friend. I ken him, and he won't be letting nothing bad happen to her."

"I suppose I could join you, as well," Ja'Baal admits some-what reluctantly.

Li'andra smiles sweetly up at Bruce as she reaches out and gives his arm a supportive squeeze. From her seat between Bruce and Aine, I've watched her flit back and forth between the two of them throughout the entire meeting, doing her best to comfort and reassure. Yeah, Griz's mom is pretty awesome. And poor Aine. She lost her brother, found him, and then lost him again all in the span of a couple of years. She needs a mother figure right now, and Li'andra is perfect.

"No!" Minova suddenly snaps, shocking the shit out of everyone by jumping up out of her chair and banging her bony fist on the table. "I cannot allow this. It's far too danger-ous. I will not risk any harm to our most valued leaders, not for such a hopeless endeavor."

She gives Horok and Ja'Baal moony-eyes, then slides her oily gaze to everyone else. "I don't mean to be cruel, but you must understand. We here as leaders must face the awful facts. We know the shuttle exploded only a few clicks from Fisan. It was out of control and bleeding passengers into space the entire way back to Tarilax before it finally crashed in the most dangerous section of the jungle. It pains me to say that the odds of finding anyone alive at all are miniscule."

We here as leaders? Who the hell does she think she is? And

119

why would she say shit like that to us right now? She doesn't mean to be cruel, my ass. *Pfft.* That bitch is heartless.

"We must all be brave right now," she continues. "Lachlin and Emily would have wanted us to remain strong. Let's not lose even more precious lives by having our bravest and brightest participate in such a needless wild buffagoose chase." Her eyes settle on Horok.

"Nonsense," Ja'Baal replies. "There's a chance they may still be alive, no matter how small."

"Enough of a chance to risk losing your life? Or, ValElysia forbid, the life of our beloved Horok?" She turns her eyes to Horok, and Cora looks as though she may scratch them out of the bitch's head. "Is it worth even the lives of our best warriors? No, I'm sorry, it's not. There's no telling what carnivorous predators and vicious creatures might have been drawn to the bloody crash site."

Aine chokes as the others around the table gasp and growl.

"I mean to say, there's just no need for all of this," Minova continues. "I wouldn't dream of subjecting you all to the potentially awful scene at the . . . er . . . landing site. I'm afraid I really must insist. My sire has already assembled a team of elite guards, and they are waiting for me at the loading bay. I'll be overseeing the mission myself and will keep you advised of our status once we've reached the coordinates."

Nordric shakes his head, his fists clenching on the tabletop. "Look here. You don't speak—"

"Thank you, Minova," Councilor Irston interrupts, leering at Nordric. "I'm sure everyone here recognizes your bravery and your willingness to put yourself in danger to recover the rem—uh . . . their friends and family. I think you should get started post-haste."

I cut my eyes at Eff. What the hell are they trying to pull? Minova couldn't care less about Emily or Lachlin or any of the rest of us, except maybe Horok or Councilman Ja'Baal. Like the old song goes, if that chick's lips are moving, she's lying. Eff glances at me, and I can see he's thinking the same thing.

"Horok," Cora finally speaks. "Surely, you don't agree—"

"Let me remind you, Your Majesty," Councilor Irston interrupts as he addresses Horok, his puckered lips resembling a butthole. "These are the same elite guardsmen that your sire hand-selected and trained for the Salemni recon mission last rotation. I'm sure he would no doubt expect your support of my daughter's initiative in light of their qualifications and experience."

Horok glares at Irston. "I don't think—"

"Especially with such a need to secure next week's vote on the Marsonium miners' minimum wage act," Irston hastily adds.

Well, that weasel-ly little bastard. I know blackmail when I hear it, especially when he didn't even try to hide it. He didn't even make an attempt to cover it up. No veiled threats here. And we all know how much the miners' act means to Horok and Cora.

Horok sits up straight, his lips pressed together tightly. I slide my hand under the table and squeeze Eff's thigh, digging my nails into his flesh to keep from jumping over the table and strangling the asshole.

"Aaah!" Eff yells, and I realize I probably squeezed him a little harder than I meant to. Everyone turns to look at him. "Uh . . . .*ahem* . . . I meant to say I'm glad we got that settled. Come, Lisa. I'll see you home."

Say what? Has he lost his marbles? No way I can leave here without taking someone's liver home in a doggy bag.

He stands, wraps his fingers around my upper arm, and gives me the *eye*. I know the eye. The eye means shut-up and do as I'm told. We're up to something. I nod and force myself to smile politely at the others as I push back my chair and get up.

"Right. So I guess I'll see you guys at home, then." Maggie and Shauna nod, looking at me as if I've lost my mind. "Cora, could I speak with you outside for a minute, please?"

"Of course," Cora says, trying to act normal as she excuses herself and makes her way over to the door.

"About the miners' act," Horok says, leaning toward Irston and Ja'Baal and providing us with a much-needed distraction. "Am I understanding then that we can expect your support when it comes up for vote next Marsday?"

We don't hang around to hear the rest. I grab Cora's arm and drag her out into the hallway where Eff is already waiting.

"So what are we going to do, then?" Cora stands, her fists propped on her hips. "That bitch is up to something."

I look at Eff expectantly, and he does not disappoint.

"She most definitely is. I'm just not sure what yet. You can bet her dear old sire is at the bottom of it, though. My ship is built for speed. We can beat them to the crash site," he says, then looks at me. "We'll leave now, Amazon, and wait for them at the coordinates. If we use the cloaking, they won't even know we're there. Maybe they'll give themselves away."

I love this scheming blue hunk of handsome.

"Great. But come with me to Horok's office first," Cora says.

"Uh . . . Kind of in a hurry here, Commander," I reply, frankly surprised that she doesn't know this already.

She smiles at me. "I know, but Horok has a new holo-vid prototype that he's helping to test for the military. If you can get it on the bridge of her ship, you won't have to guess at what they're up to. You'll be able to witness it first-hand."

I love this evil gestating genius, too.

Leaving the conference center, Epherus and I split up. He heads for the ship, and I make my way to Slip Seventy-Three where the Irstonorca is preparing to depart on a priority rescue mission.

Chapter Seventeen

Epherus

I pace back and forth on the bridge, my stomach in knots waiting for my Amazon to return. I don't like this. My hearts feel funny, my horns are achy, and I can't seem to get my quills to relax.

That vessel belongs to a high-ranking government official, a Tarilean Council member. If she's caught, they could detain her, lock her up in a cell, torture her, even. She could be charged with spying or treason or some other trumped up felonious wokshite. I should have gone in her place, whether she liked it or not. She would have gotten over it. Eventually. I could have found some reason or some way to get inside the ship to see that conniving femki. I could have already slipped in, creeped past Irston's warriors, planted the bug, and been back by now.

"Let's go! Hurry!" Lisa comes barreling onto the bridge, her face red and sweaty.

Fuck. Are they chasing her? I make a dive for my captain's chair and begin entering our launch codes and hyperdrive coordinates. My fingers fly over the keyboard as I type in the lockdown sequence next, securing the ship and preparing for takeoff. Once I'm comfortable that Lisa is safe and we're good for departure, I allow myself a beat to look at her.

"Did you get it?"

"Oh, yeah. I got it, all right." She chuckles as she settles into the navigation chair and begins to fiddle with a small cylindrical device. It's the receiver dock for the holo-bug.

"That idiot didn't have a clue. She honestly thinks we believe she's doing this as some kind of noble humanitarian effort. Or would that be a Tarileanitarian effort?"

"She is just as obtuse and self-serving as her sire." I shake my head with disgust and turn around to engage the cloaking mechanism. "Was he with her?"

"Who? Councilor Irston? No, she was by herself. Unless, of course, you count the dozen or so warriors she has with her."

Normally, I don't have any problem getting a read on Irston or the other corrupt Council members. I know better than most just how unscrupulous they can be. I've been contracted by several of them in the past for small jobs like taking out a city alderman or maiming a businessman who refuses to get involved with the complex political agendas of the Council. All of these politicorporate megalomaniacs have their own personal agendas, too. Irston has one now, and, whatever it is, he's using his own daughter to carry it out.

"Buckle up," I tell my Amazon. "We'll hover just on the other side of the atmosphere while I scan the primary trade route frequencies and get a lock on them. I don't know what the range is on that holo-bug. We may have to follow closely if you want imaging, as well as audio."

"Gah!" Frustrated, she slaps at the radio in her hand. "I don't know how to do this. I need Emily. This is her fucking job, her area of expertise. This is what she does. Dammit, she needs to be here."

I watch as my Amazon seems to shrink right in front of me, then her eyes begin to leak. Her shoulders shake as she lowers her head into her hands, hiding her face from me. She's crying, something human females tend to do when they feel extreme emotion. According to Lachlin, it's the male's job to figure out which emotion is driving it and then address it accordingly.

I can do this. Is she sad? Angry? Happy? I frown, too distracted to try and solve a complex puzzle like emotions right now. I don't like this. I don't like it all.

"Amazon," I say, using my sternest voice even though my hearts pinch with every new tear she secretes. "Make your eyes stop leaking."

"I'm sorry," she says, sniffing and swiping at her cheeks. The corners of her mouth lift weakly in a pitiful excuse for a smile. "I'm okay. I'm just being a wimpy little bitch."

I set the carbotrister alignments to thirty degrees left of zero degrees past the exit, then turn my chair around to face her.

"Listen to me," I warn. "No one slanders or disparages the mate of Epherus Zinto, not even the mate of Epherus Zinto. My Amazon is no wimpy bitch."

The shock on her face is no more than the shock registered on my own. I mean, never before have I ever referred to myself in the third person. The words just poured out unbidden. My mate. Lisa, my Amazon, is my fated one.

I should have known by the squeezing in my chest, the constant ache of my horns, and the persistent half-mast position of my quills. Not to mention the intransigent state of painful arousal or this nervous feeling that makes me want to run away and run toward her at the same time whenever I see her. I thought I was going insane.

"Little Amazon, you are my amavi compar, my fated mate."

The words taste right on my tongue, they sound right spilling past my lips, and the knowledge feels right in my soul, warming me like a claffer-hide blanket.

She stares at me for a moment unblinking, then nods slowly, her eyes once again lit with emotion. Lachlin was correct—choosing the right one can be difficult. Pride? Love? I smile and hold out my hand.

"Give me the device."

She hands me the holo-bug in her hand and observes as I secure it to the communication port. I work slowly so she can watch and learn how to operate the ship's com devices. If she's going to be my navigator and first mate, and she definitely is, she needs to know how to do this.

"Once you have these leads connected—" I point to the blue and white wires, "—then all you have to do is flip this switch."

" . . . *and they don't know anything, Montavi.*"

Minova's high-pitched, whiny voice suddenly fills the bridge. Lisa gasps and claps her hands together.

"That's perfect!" she proclaims.

My Amazon perks up immediately, smiling from ear-to-ear as she pulls two blasters and three laserblades from different compartments of her uniform and lays them on top of the console.

"What are you doing?"

"Weapons check," she chirps happily as she begins to disassemble the blasters one at a time. "I need to get me one of those molecular disbanders, too. Do you have an extra one I can use?"

I narrow my eyes and watch her. She's acting strangely, but I can't quite put my finger on why. "Yes, in the armory on the lower level. I'll get it for you when we land. So, where's the holo-image?"

"Uh . . . the holo-image?"

"Yes. I thought this thing provided both holo-vid and audio surveillance?" The apparatus is so small, you can supposedly place it in any unobstructed location in the room, and no one would even notice it.

"Oh, yeah, that. I couldn't really get it into a good spot for imaging." She shrugs like it's no big deal.

Hm. I thought that was the whole point of this prototype?

The whole reason Cora gave it to her. Just about anywhere inside the room would have been a good spot. "What do you mean? Where did you put it?"

"I . . . um . . . Well, I may have panicked just a little bit," she says, taking her bottom lip between her teeth.

I sigh loudly. "Alright. What did you do?"

"Nothing, really. I was about to place it on one of the navigation consoles when she turned around too fast and startled me. I may have accidentally dropped it."

"Dropped it?"

"Yeah, but this is working just fine, so it doesn't matter. We don't need to see her so long as we can hear her. Right?"

I stare at her as I ponder what it is she doesn't want to tell me. This is difficult. Normally, I'd just tie someone up and pull out their fangs or start yanking claws until they gave me the information I wanted. Perhaps I'm not asserting my authority as dominantly as I should be? Perhaps my Amazon needs some punishment?

"Tell me where you dropped the holo-bug, Amazon."

She sighs and tosses her laserblade onto the table. It lands in front of her with a clatter as she begins to fidget with the equalization controls on the com system.

"In her cup," she sighs.

"In her cup? Did she drink it?"

"Sort of." She gives me a guilty smile as I sit in stunned silence. "But think of the bright side, Eff. If she leaves the bridge, we'll still be able to hear her. Not only that, we'll be able to report in our findings what the effects of human . . . er . . . Tarilean ingestion are on the prototype's capabilities. I mean, just listen to that. Clear as a bell! I bet they never tested that in the lab."

I want to argue, but I can't. She's right. No Tarilean in his right mind would have agreed to ingesting a potentially radioactive Marsonium-based spy device for the sake of a trial.

And the audio does sound crystal clear.

"*I'm telling you they suspect something.*" Montavi, Minova's personal guard, says. "*That human has never ventured a visit here before. She was up to something. We should do a full sweep of the ship.*"

"*Who cares if they suspect something? They can't prove a thing, and there aren't any witnesses to say otherwise. If any evidence did somehow survive the crash, or witnesses, for that matter, we'll take care of it when we get there.*"

"*Unless they've already escaped. They could be traveling to the capitol right now. With the serum!*"

"*Come now, Montavi. Surely, you don't think anyone could have survived that crash? You're as frizzucking gullible as they are. And even if they did, which they didn't, no civilians or off-worlders could make it through the Zaothe jungle alive.*"

"*We'll see soon enough, I guess. Let's just hope the vaccine survived.*"

"*That idiot Czaren. I told him Rowark would never hand it over willingly. He was way too 'Tarilean' for that. Him and his damn warrior code of honor.*"

Czaren? As in the enforcer of the Aurelian king? I can't believe my fucking ears. Why was she speaking with Czaren about a Tarilean warrior? And why was he onboard the shuttle with Lachlin and Emily? And what the fuck does any of this have to do with a serum or vaccine?

"*Do you think he rigged the serum with an explosive device?*" Montavi asks.

"*I find it hard to believe he would have risked the lives of everyone onboard that shuttle, but I'm not sure what else could have happened.*"

"*Could the humans have something to do with it?*"

She growls. "*Possibly. They seem to frizzuck everything they touch.*"

Montavi sighs loudly. "*What if the serum isn't recovered? Will we still get our money?*"

"That's the five-hundred besdando dollar question, now, isn't it? We lived up to our end of the bargain. We delivered the time, the place, and the courier to Oaryundu. We did everything except steal the frizzucking serum ourselves and hand it over to him. I want my money."

Sweet goddess! Oaryundu? The crowned prince of Aurelia? I glance nervously at my Amazon to see if she understands the significance of what we're hearing. Does she recognize the name Oaryundu? Is so, I can't tell. Her face is blank, giving nothing away as her fingers work like lightning to assemble the various weapon parts scattered on the table.

"Well, look on the bright side, my lady. At least, that's one less human female we have to deal with. And Ja'Baal is free and clear. You could be mated within a fortnight."

"You think?" She chuckles. *"Maybe, but now, I wonder if I may have given up on Horok a little too soon. He looked so miserable tonight, saddled with that . . . that human whore and her pack of hybrid brats."*

"Perhaps we can take out another contract with the Aurelians?"

"You don't think it's too soon?"

"Of course not. No one wants those worthless humans on Tarilax. They'll only pollute and weaken our bloodlines. And to have one mated to our king? Tarileans will thank you for purging the royal house."

My poor Amazon.

"You may be right. Let's see about our money first. Then, we'll take care of the humans."

There's some rustling and the whooshing of doors as Minova leaves the bridge, then nothing but her faint echoing footsteps down the hallway. I look at my mate, concerned and quite frankly, stunned by what we just heard. Somehow, she's already finished reassembling every one of the weapons that she had broken down earlier. Still, she has not spoken a word, which makes me nervous. She stands up and reaches into her inside pocket.

I watch now as she silently flicks open each laserblade, examines it, and snaps it shut again with a swish of her wrist. Satisfied, she deposits each weapon back into one of the inner pockets of her uniform. Finally, she takes the last blaster in her hand and ejects the cell pack, pops it out and checks the charge, then slaps it shut against her thigh.

She aims at a point across the room and says, "That bitch is mine."

Chapter Eighteen

Emily

"What is that?" I cup my hand over my brows to block the sun from my eyes as I squint up at the sky.

"It's a ship," Lachlin says, turning around and glancing behind us.

My heart speeds up, and for the first time in several hours, I think maybe we're going to be okay.

"A rescue ship? Should we turn around and go back? What do we do?" I'm practically vibrating with excitement.

Unfortunately, it doesn't last long. My spirits sag when Lachlin shakes his head.

"No. It's too far away. We'd never make it back in time, if we made it back at all."

No, no, no!

"How about a signal or something? Maybe we can get a big blaze going, or shoot off a flare? I don't know, maybe light a monkey on fire?"

He gives me a 'look'. You know the type, the God-grant-me-strength-to-deal-with-this-idiot type of look, which kind of surprises me considering we've just spent all morning back at the hidden grotto making love and whispering like lovesick teenagers.

"We should have stayed near the ship," I grumble, frustrated and near the end of my rope.

"It wasn't safe there out in the open by the river," he says. "Too much animal traffic because of the water. Besides, we can't burn the jungle down just to get a ship's attention, and I'm afraid I'm fresh out of flares."

I must look like I'm about to cry or explode because he frowns, then grabs me and pulls me to him, hugging me and kissing me on top of my head.

"It's going to be okay, Duchess, I swear. I'm not going to let anything happen to you. We just need to keep heading north, and we'll make it to one of the villages."

"'Kay." I sniff, nodding against his chest.

Gosh, I'm turning into a whiny bitch. I need to suck it up and keep going. I'm a strong, vibrant, resourceful woman. I shouldn't need Lachlin to take care of me like I'm a child.

"I'm ready." I step back, nod, and brush my hair out of my face. "Let's do this. I want to go home and take a hot shower. Maybe order a good meal and veg out on some daytime soaps. Surprisingly, the one called "As the Tarilax Turns" is not bad at all."

He smiles, winks at me, then slaps me on the ass before heading off down the trail. I feel like I should be holding a whistle or a football. We walk in silence for a while, Lachlin handing me berries and nuts occasionally, until we pass by the biggest Haeplon tree I've ever seen. There's a huge one outside my bedroom window at the palace, but even that one is not as big as this one. I step up to it, craning my neck to look up through the branches.

"Hey! Hang on a minute." I shout at Lachlin.

He stops, turns around, and gives me a curious look. "What is it?"

Instead of answering, I leap off the ground, grab hold of the lowest limb, and hang there for a moment while I make sure it will hold my weight. Once I'm convinced it will, I throw my leg over it and swing myself up. I sit there on the thick limb smiling at Lachlin. I've never seen a tree that begged for someone to climb it like this one does. I couldn't have designed it any better with its spongy bark that almost clings back to me and branches wide enough to fit even my generous ass.

"Stay right there," I call down to him.

In minutes, I've managed to reach the very top. I brace my back against the tree and look toward the spot by the river where I think we crashed. There it is! A ship. I can barely make it out in the distance, but it's there. I can see the suns reflecting off its hull.

"There's the ship! They're at the crash site!" I yell to Lachlin. "I can see them. Well, I can see their ship."

"What about villages? Can you see anything to the North or West?" he calls up to me.

I look all around, not wanting to admit that I don't know which way north or west really is. Doesn't matter, anyway, since I can't see anything except trees and mountains in any direction I turn. But, wait a minute. What the fuck is that?

"Holy shit," I gasp. My throat tightens as I take in the scene in front of me.

Far off to my right just a little — northwest, maybe? Whatever the hell direction that is, the trees are swaying, the leaves are shaking, and there's a stampede of animals heading in our direction. I catch glimpses of them here and there, my sight spotty through the thick trees, but they're obviously panicked, running for their lives and flying in all directions, except for one. But that's not the freaky part. They're running from something. Something that looks a lot like a . . . a . . . freaking Tyrannosaurus Rex? Some kind of giant lizard?

The thing is as big as a skyscraper, its teeth as tall as small trees even from this distance. It tosses its big, oblong head around as though it's frustrated, snapping its huge maw open and shut and roaring out at the jungle. At least, I think it's roaring. If I strain my ears, I can barely hear it over the gusts of howling wind up here.

I don't know how I could have missed it on my first sweep. Its head is shaped, well, like a lizard, like you'd expect a T-Rex's head to be shaped. Its skin is a dirty orange color, and even from here, I can tell it's thick and plated like armor, rough-looking the way a crocodile and a rhino and a dragon hide might look if you mixed all three together.

Fuck, maybe it is a dragon? All those myths could have been founded in truth, from these space creatures. Or maybe Godzilla is real, too?

Sweet baby budda, it's Dragozilla! A godzillasaurus!

"Aack!" I lose my balance trying to scoot further away from the damn thing and topple off the limb backwards. I don't even really mind that I'm plunging to my death so long as Godzilla Rex is nowhere nearby. I reach out to grasp a branch that just slapped me in the face and miss it, only to have it reach down and grab me by the wrist instead.

"Duchess! Are you all right?" Lachlin has already started running up after me.

I may not be falling anymore, but I just saw a real-life dragon dinosaur, and a tree just reached out and yanked me from the jaws of death. I'm a far cry from being all right.

"Wow. Thank you," I whisper to the tree as I pet the velvety branch that just saved my life. I'd rather Lachlin not hear me and decide that I've totally lost the rest of my marbles. At least, not until he confirms that Godzilla, the orange-yellow dragonasaur, is real.

"Duchess!"

I look down to see Lachlin's extremely beautiful, extremely distraught face looking up at me.

"Lachlin! We have to go! Now! That way!" I point down at the ground, in the opposite direction of the beast, then try to resume my descent down the tree.

"Wait. Stop." He reaches out to grab me as I struggle to shimmy past. "Hang on a minute. Are you okay?"

He pulls me into him, locking his arms around me as he leans back against the tree.

"No, I'm not. We have to go," I insist, pushing against him and trying to wiggle out of his iron hold.

"Jesus, Duchess. Calm down. You're shaking like a leaf," he says, squeezing me tighter.

I pause, take a deep breath, and look him in the eye. "Lachlin, you have to listen to me. There's a damn Godzillasaurus heading straight for us. I've seen all seventeen of those old dinosaur movies on Earth, and I'm telling you, we're about to star in Jurassic Fucked."

He squints at me. "What are you talking about?"

"Just go look!" I point to the top of the tree. "Hurry, though, because we've got to get out of here."

I force myself to stand there and wait as Lachlin climbs his way to the top and perches on the same limb where I sat before. He cups his hand above his brow and scans over the horizon.

"What are you talking about, Duchess? I don't see—"

Suddenly, he stops, jerks backward, and nearly keels over backwards off the branch, the same way I did.

"Holy Shit!" he yells. "What the fuck is that?"

CHAPTER NINETEEN

Lisa

"It's a fucking T-Rex," I tell Eff, my face smashed up against the window as I watch the ginormous lizard stomping around the jungle below. "No, no. It's bigger than a T-Rex. It's a twenty-story Raptorsaurus. An Enormasaurus. In fact, I don't think they've even invented a word for something like that yet."

Eff chuckles. Fucking chuckles! "It's a Leatherback Lacertilia."

Lacertilia? As in lizard? I guess that fits. It's that or a damn dragon, except I don't see any wings, and it hasn't spewed forth any fiery lava or freezing snot.

"How the hell can you be so calm? If that thing decides to turn around head into the city, we're all screwed. There'd be no place to hide from it, no safe spot it couldn't get to or stomp into smithereens."

"That *thing* will not enter the city, my amavi. It hates artificial light. They aren't even fond of sunlight. They're nocturnal by nature, and I'm surprised it's even up and moving about."

He called me his *amavi* again. I nearly sigh every time he says it. I know what an amavi is. Cora is Horok's amavi, and Aine is Griz's amavi. We call them soulmates back on Earth, but no one back there really believes in them anymore. We stopped searching for our soulmates a long, long time ago. But out here in the depths of space, everyone believes in them. They dream of finding the other half of their soul, and when they do, they cherish and adore that person forever. They don't just pay lip service until they get bored, either. No, they dedicate their entire lives to their dying breaths loving and treasuring their amavi compars. Their fated mates.

"Try not to worry, my love. These animals never leave the confines of the jungle. In fact, it's almost unheard of to see one even this close. The Lacertilia been around forever. Or at least, eons longer than we have, and never in recorded history has there ever been an account of one venturing into a civilized township."

"Hm. This one looks like it might have rabies," I tell him as I squint down at the vicious demon-lizard. It reaches down and snags a wild elephant-looking animal and chomps it down like a little snack. "Shouldn't we call Horok and have him send his army out to kill it? They could bring a nuclear weapon or a Marsonium bomb or something."

Eff shakes his head. "They're a protected species. The most Horok could do is try to have them drive it back toward its herd if it got too close to a township."

"On the same planet is too close in my opinion. What if it catches up with Emily or Lachlin? It's right in between them and the closest town. What're they called again? Tortillas?"

"Lacertilias. It's not like it can sneak up on them, amavi. Lachlin will make sure they keep a safe distance from it."

I sigh and rip my eyes away from the huge beast long enough to check on Eff's progress. He's still bent over the weird-looking laptop thingy, his long, thick fingers working nimbly connecting and reconnecting wires, removing and re-placing chips, and popping little fuses in and out. The longer I watch him, the more my mouth starts to water. Fuck, he looks good.

His long, dark hair is pulled back and held into place by a thin leather thong. A few wisps have worked their way loose from the ponytail and dance around his handsome face. The muscles in his arms flex and twitch as he fumbles with the awkward device, and his shoulders roll enticingly every time he flips it over or reaches for a new tool. And those lips? Oh. My. Word. The way his tongue snakes out to lick over them when he's lost in thought? I bite my own lip as my pussy clenches with need. How the hell can I be horny at a time like this?

I clear my throat and try to act normal as I casually saunter across the room and peer over his shoulder. "How's it coming?"

"I think I'm done." He picks up something that looks like a screwdriver and reattaches the cover to the laptop. "We won't lose her again. The next time they leave the ship, we'll know exactly where they go. We should test it, though."

"Tell me again how this thing works?"

"When I attach the holo-bug dock to the device, it will synchronize to the bug she ingested and allow us to track her every movement. I just take the dock, like this, and connect it right here, like so." He picks up the dock and snaps it into a UB port of some kind.

The monitor lights up with a flashing red dot. I watch as it moves slowly around the screen, proving thankfully that she's still aboard her ship.

"You did it!" I wrap my arms around his shoulders and give him an innocent hug. Or what I will call an innocent hug. No one can prove any differently. "Oh, baby, you're so good."

He doesn't say anything, but I can tell he's pleased, both with himself and with me fawning all over him. I smile and kiss his cheek. Damn, he tastes good. I do it again, letting my lips linger for a bit longer to get the full Eff effect.

"Amavi," he whispers, his hand reaching back to squeeze my butt.

I wiggle myself in between him and the table, stroking his horns as I lean into his lap. When his eyes roll back and he sighs, I reach down and relieve him of his shirt. Then, my lips get busy planting a procession of little kisses across his smooth, wide chest and up and down his neck. He drops the laptop on the table with a clatter, and his hands begin roaming up and down my arms, slowly shifting to my breasts.

"Mm," I moan as I lick a heated trail from his neck to the slight indention beneath his ear.

He groans and flexes his hips into me, his interest becoming clear as it pokes me in the stomach.

"Amazon," he rumbles, ripping my shirt over my head, then grabbing my hair and yanking it until my knees hit the floor. With me kneeling between his legs, he tilts my face to his, and I present him with my lips. He growls and takes them, making my thoughts scatter and my body thrill.

Eff kisses me with the force of a meteor storm, his hands fisting in my hair with such passion, such possession, that nothing else matters right now. He's rough and aggressive, and I love it.

My hands move frantically down his chest, my nails scratching over his rock-hard stomach until my fingers settle on the top button of his black cargo pants. *Pop*. He growls his approval against my lips, his cock so hard, it's trying to burst through his pants and jump into my hand.

Literally, I can feel his package wiggling against the palm of my hand. I work blindly at the next fasten, my fingers unzipping and tugging at it impatiently. His lips stay locked to mine as he reaches down and unhooks the last of the trouser chassis. He lifts his ass out of the chair just enough to shift them down to his ankles, dragging his shorts along with them. And then, I feel him. Not with my hands, either.

Like a floodgate had been opened, my breasts are suddenly covered with long, tentacle-like appendages, warm and soft, gliding and tickling me all over. They wrap around each breast, gently exploring as they squeeze and flick my nipples.

When one of the tips abruptly latches on to my nipple, sucking and tugging on it like a freaking vacuum cleaner, I gasp into Eff's mouth.

"Sorry. I can't control my phila when they're this excited," he says, as if it that should resolve any confusion. Then, he goes back to kissing me, his tongue laving my neck as the second tentacle latches on to my other nipple.

Phila? I feel like I should be freaking out, but honestly, I'm not. This is Eff. My Eff. My mate. This is part of him, a big part, and it's the way he's built. I accept that. More than that, I embrace it because, honestly? It feels so fucking good, I wouldn't want him any other way. And with that thought, one of his phila slides down my stomach, over my mound, and down to my slick pussy. I cry out as it tugs at my clit, then dips down through my lips and enters me.

"Eff!" I'm going to explode, and he hasn't even touched me with a normal appendage yet!

"Come, Amavi," he whispers to me, as if I needed permission or encouragement.

I come, all right. Boy, do I come. My pussy throbs and clenches around his phila while I tremble with ecstasy. Eff pulls my hair roughly, trailing kisses down my neck as his other phila stroke me all over. By the time I'm done, I'm already building up to the next one.

"We aren't done yet, Amazon," he says as he reaches down and wraps a fist around his writhing cock.

My eyes sink down to his lap, finally getting the first good look at what's going on down there. They widen with surprise when I see his big, blue dick snaking back and forth amidst a dozen writhing tentacles. Or phila, I guess. My eyes nearly cross trying to take it all in. There's a small nub that rests on top of his cock, and the first thing I think of is a shark fin. The tip bends and strains toward me as Eff holds it back, and the theme song from the movie Jaws keeps rolling through my head.

It's weird, sure, but it's Eff. It's beautiful.

"Oh, Eff," I breathe as I lower my face to his lap.

I take him in my mouth until my lips rest against the edges of his fist, and I begin to work him with my tongue. The bump on top is hard, but flexible like cartilage. I flick it a few times, then drop my head and hollow my cheeks, sucking like a maniac.

"Fuck!" he bellows, letting go of his cock to grip the arms of his chair. His breath hisses and becomes erratic.

Interesting. Excited as I am, I manage to take in a lot more of him than I thought I could, cataloging each reaction. But my tongue keeps returning to that very interesting nubbin on top of his cock. I lick and lave it like he did my clit. I don't know if that's what it is, a male clit, but he gasps every time I suck on it.

His cock begins to drill in and out of my mouth excitedly, which seems strange when I realize that Eff's hips aren't moving. Now, it's propelling itself toward the back of my throat, only pausing when I gag. But even that doesn't deter it for long, and soon, it takes on a punishing pace. His phila become agitated, wiggling wildly over my breasts, my face, my lips. I open my mouth wider and take one of them inside, too, sucking and licking it with his cock.

"Godsdamn!" Eff suddenly shouts, his entire body tensing. The sound of his chair arm cracking is like a gunshot echoing through the room.

He lets go of the chair, grabs the back of my head, and pulls me into him hard as his cock explodes into my throat. His phila vibrate and hum as they pluck roughly at my nipples and breasts. Then, as soon as I swallow the first mouthful of his seed, and after I think I've seen everything, I'm hit with the fucking mack daddy of orgasms. I come so hard, it makes my teeth hurt, and I nearly choke.

After he deposits about a liter of seed into my stomach, and I stop convulsing, he melts back into the chair and sighs. Reaching down, he grabs my chin and lifts my face until he meets my eyes.

"Amavi," he pants, his eyes still black and hooded.

"What the fuck just happened?" Not the most romantic post-coital pillow talk, I know, but what can I say? I'm shell-shocked and just experienced the most violent, bone-jarring orgasm of my life. And I'd like to repeat it as soon as possible. "I never dreamed I could come that hard, and you weren't even touching me down there."

He chuckles. "That would be the skeaf."

"Skeaf?"

"Yeah, it's a unique chemical secreted by Aurelian males and passed through our seed. It has that effect on females when ingested during sex."

Seriously?

"Well, lucky you." I giggle. "Looks like there's a boatload of blow jobs in your future!"

CHAPTER TWENTY

Emily

I shake my head and sigh.

"So, do you believe me now? I don't know what that giant lizard-looking thing is, and frankly, I don't care. I just want it to be in a different hemisphere. Now, come on and let's get the hell out of here."

A minute later, Lachlin drops down from the tree and lands beside me. He swivels his head around, a thoughtful look on his face as he rubs his stubbly chin with his finger. I stay quiet and give him time to come up with a plan. After witnessing Dinozilla, I don't think I trust my own judgement enough to come up with one on my own. Somehow running off through the trees while I fling my arms around in the air screaming 'Oh, fuck, we're going to die' just doesn't seem very helpful at this stage. Unfortunately, it's the only plan I can think of.

"I'm not as worried about Barney as I am those stampedes," he says. "If we get caught up in that, we'll be crushed into dust."

"Yeah, but if we get caught up by Barney, we'll be chewed into mush and turned into dinoshit. So, what's your preference?"

"It's big, but it moves slow. It's also loud, so we'll have plenty of warning if it gets any closer."

"I'll have to trust your judgement on that. Now, which way do we go?" *Please don't point in Godzillasaur's direction.*

144

He takes a deep breath and exhales loudly, then points at a mountain peak to our left. "There. That gets us to higher ground and out of the way of the stampede. We may be able to spot a village or a road, even."

I squint at the point he's considering and muse. "Yes, but won't we be trapped if Barney decides to follow us?"

He opens his mouth to reply when a gigantic gorilla with the head of a rhinoceros bursts through the thick, yellow brush beside us and plows right into us. Lachlin goes sprawling several feet through the air like a rag doll. His limp body hurtles through a wall of brambles on the other side of the Haeplon tree and disappears.

"Lachlin!" My heart feels like it's being ripped out of my chest and fed to a flock of baby pterodactyls. Then, the beast starts to growl and make chomping noises at me.

I manage to squeak out a weird noise that sounds like the culmination of sorrow, shock, surprise, dread and extreme terror. I can't decide if I should stop, drop, and roll or run like my ass is on fire. Should I lower my eyes in subservience, or glower at it and try to fake my dominance? Is this where I'm supposed to put my head between my knees and kiss my ass goodbye? Play dead? Put up my dukes?

Its beady black eyes lock onto me, and it begins to snort and snarl and thump fists the size of Halloween pumpkins against its chest.

"Well, shit. What am I? A fucking monkey magnet?"

I don't have any more time to consider the right maneuver as it begins to creep forward, saliva dripping from its lips, and its fucking four-inch fangs glistening at me.

"Nice goroserous," I coo, my feet inching backwards. "Just stay calm now."

My eyes dart around the ground looking for something to use as a weapon. All I find is a stick. A fucking stick. It's better than nothing, I guess. Slowly, I reach down to pick it up. Just as my fingers curl around the thick twig, the goroserous goes insane.

It throws its enormous arms in the air and bellows so loud, I think I go temporarily deaf. Or I turn into one of those little feinting goats and just topple over all stiff-legged and drooling. Or more than likely, I just trip over my own feet and hit the ground. Hard. I shake my head trying to clear away the blinding panic, narrowing my eyes at the beast and clutching my twig while I shake it at him. I feel like an angry pet owner with a rolled up newspaper. Bad goroserous. Bad.

With a loud cry, Lachlin returns abruptly, vaulting over the bushes like a fucking gazelle and landing directly in front of me.

"Get away from her, you hairy bastard!" He throws his fists into the air and dances back and forth like a heavyweight contender.

The goroserous howls and leaps straight toward him. My guts curdle, my asshole puckers, and tears fill my eyes as I watch the love of my life prepare to die. Again. To protect me.

Suddenly, the trees split open in front of me, and a spider head the size of a fucking Humvee pops through. It shoots a milky white web from two big holes beneath its chin and snags the goroserous right out of the air only millimeters away from Lachlin. The goroserous lands flat on his back a short ways from the spider, howling and flailing as the sticky gossamer wraps tighter around him. I watch with horrified relief as the spider reels him in like a fish on a hook.

"Duchess!"

Lachlin races over to me, scoops me off the ground, and throws me over his shoulder as we haul ass back into the jungle. Lachlin, the love of my life.

I don't even bitch about being upside down or my head banging against his rock-hard ass with every step he takes or the way he's jostling me so much, my stomach threatens to eject the nuts and berries I had for lunch. I'm so happy he's alive, that we're alive, I just kiss him everywhere my lips land as my face jostles and bangs against him.

I don't know how far we run before he finally stops and slides me off his shoulder, his chest heaving in and out as he crumbles to his knees. I'd love to comfort him, but I fear I'm in worse shape than he is. Flopping out spread-eagle on the ground, I wait until the sky stops spinning, and I then sit up and crawl over to him.

"Lachlin, sweetie." I press my hand against his cheek as I glance around checking for anything that might stomp us, poke us, bite us, or wrap us in a gossamer blanket. The coast looks clear, for now.

We've managed to find one of the few fields scattered throughout the dense jungle, and while I don't like the fact that we're wide out in the open, at least nothing can burst through the trees, leap out of a bush, or sneak up on us here. What I wouldn't give for a Holiday Inn right about now.

"I'm. *Pant.* Okay. *Pant.* Just give. *Pant.* Me a second. *Pant.*"

I reach for the medical kit to grab some water and realize that it's gone. Shit. It must have fallen off while I was riding upside down through the jungle. Hesitating for only a second, I grab the one off Lachlin's belt and uncap it.

"Here. Take a drink."

He doesn't argue, snatching it from my hand and tipping it straight to his lips. He takes a couple of big gulps and hands it back, swiping his lips with the back of his arm. I look at the bottle for a second, tempted, but then put the cap on it and clip it back to his belt loop. Here we go again, rationing water until we can find the next decent pool to hydrate.

I look up at the sky. The suns are high, and I can tell it's late in the afternoon now, which means we're going to need to find cover soon. I stand up and look around for the mountain peaks we'd decided to shelter in, but now, they're way off to our left.

"We're off course," he says, getting his wind back. He rests an arm on his bended knee and shakes his head in irritation. "I took off like a fool in the wrong direction back there. All I could think about was getting you out of there and away from that fucking spider."

"Well, I'm glad you did. I freaking hate spiders. And those were little ones. That titantula one was like a nightmare on steroids, except I guess we're lucky it showed up when it did."

He chuckles. "Titantula. I think you found a fitting name for it."

I smile back at him, hoping to lighten the mood and assure him that I'm not at all angry about going in the wrong direction. Hell, I never wanted to go up there on that mountain in the first place.

"I'm really missing our secret garden right about now." I sigh wistfully. "Maybe we can find another one to stay in tonight?"

"That'd be nice, but there's only seven of them like that in the entire universe. So I doubt we'll run across anymore on this trip." He reaches down and pushes himself up off the ground, swiping at the dirt on his pants. "I'll be happy if we can just find a cave or something safe to bed down in for the night."

He reaches down a hand to pull me up, but before I can take it or say anything else, the ground beneath my ass begins to rumble and shake. Eyes wide with disbelief, I look at Lachlin.

"An earthquake? Seriously? What next? A tsunami? An active volcano?"

Frowning, he pulls me to my feet. "That's no earthquake, sweetheart."

Then, we hear a roar that's so loud and so scary, the hair

on the back of my neck stands up.

"That's Barney," he says.

CHAPTER TWENTY-ONE

Lachlin

I watch as all the color drains out of Duchess' face. She tries to speak but only manages to gurgle. She's terrified, not to mention exhausted. If we ever get out of this, I vow to spend the rest of my life making it up to her, if she'll let me. I'd love nothing better right now than to take her in my arms and hold her until Barney is nothing but a bad memory. Unfortunately, we just don't have that luxury right now.

"Come on." I give her hand a good tug to get her feet moving. "We need to keep going."

The ground rumbles every few seconds as we hightail it across the little pasture. I can't tell exactly where Barney is, but it feels like he's close and getting closer by the second. Of all the warm-blooded menu items for him to choose from here in the jungle, why the hell is he following us?

I wasn't lying when I told Duchess that I didn't think the big lizard was able to move very fast, but that didn't mean that he's not faster than we are. We need to get off this open field and back under some quick cover. With that thought, I speed up until we're moving along at a brisk jog. I grab Duchess' hand to make sure she stays with me.

"That way." I jerk my head toward a clearing in the brush up ahead just as a thunderous boom rolls over the field behind us.

"Shit!" Duchess yelps.

Her feet seem to shift gears, and damn if she doesn't drop

my hand and zip right past me.

"Duchess! Over here!"

I duck into a thin line of trees and start beating a path with my bare hands, ripping vines and branches out of the way as we go. I can feel the ground trembling with every step Barney takes as we burrow through the brush and brambles.

"We need to move faster," she says, diving beneath a long tree trunk and belly-crawling through a particularly gnarly cluster of stickers.

Her ass shines from beneath her dress, and I stand there for a second paralyzed, watching her slither and squirm her way through the obstacle course in front of us. I scowl, Barney's heavy footsteps coming so close together now that I can't even take time out to enjoy this magnificent view. Selfish prick. I swallow, try to push all erotic thoughts out of my head, and drop to my hands and knees to follow her.

We make it out of the bramble patch with most of our skin intact, continuing on at a fast trot for what feels like miles. We take turns stealing the lead from each other while the ground shakes and rattles until, finally, the mountain comes into view. Unfortunately, the light is growing dimmer by the minute, and when I glance up at the sky again, I know there's no way we're going to make it to the top before dark.

"It's coming!" Duchess shouts when she streaks past me again, leaving a trail of dust in her wake as she runs straight up the side of a jagged cliff.

Damn this wretched beast. Glancing behind me, I see the trees shaking, hear the wide trunks cracking, and I know he's only a short distance away. I put on some speed, too, catching the side of the cliff at a dead run and letting momentum carry me up as far as possible before I hit all fours.

I cling to the rock face like I'm fucking Spiderman, looking up to see Duchess' pretty ass smiling down at me from about half-way up the cliffside. She's a really good climber.

"Hurry up!"

She turns around, calling down to me, and I can tell from her shaky voice and the way her eyes widen as they lock on to something behind me that we have company.

Before I have a chance to turn around and look, the mountain explodes into a full-on nine on the Richter scale. I glance behind me to see that Barney has done the same thing we did, hit the cliff at a full-on run and latched on like a tree frog. I start climbing again even with my eyes still glued to the giant lizard below us. That was my next mistake.

If I'd been paying attention or if the suns' light hadn't already begun to fade on us, I might have seen that the rock wasn't stable enough to hold me. I probably would have avoided putting my foot directly on top of it or leaning all my body weight on it. But of course, I wasn't, and I didn't, so I did. The next thing I know, I'm sliding down a big blue mountain on my face right toward the gaping, salivating maw of death directly below me.

I kick and claw and scrabble desperately for any purchase I can get, which turns out to be none, actually. My face feels like it's sliding down a wall of jagged glass, and I cough and sputter, spitting dirt and grass as I go. Somehow, I manage to flip around on my back, which does nothing to slow me down. At least, I'm not eating dirt anymore.

"Lachlin! Get down!"

I hear Duchess scream and hope like hell she turns around so she doesn't have to witness what's about to happen. After everything I've been through, I never dreamed it would end like this, being eaten by a fucking lizard. I sure don't want her having to carry around an image like that in her beautiful head for the rest of her life.

The knowledge of his supper being served up on a platter by the mountain must please Barney greatly because I swear I hear him sigh right before he bellows out his gratitude. Wait.

That's not gratitude. Those are big fucking rocks bouncing off his giant reptilian head. Suddenly, one whizzes past, clipping me on the ear, and I start to hope that maybe one might take me out before Barney does.

"Look out, Lachlin!"

I flip over again, not wanting to see myself slide into Barney's gullet. I squint my eyes and spit out a mouthful of dirt, already resigned to my fate. So I barely notice the giant shadow that passes over the entire length of my body. Barney notices, though.

He trumpets one last long roar before a thick, meaty thud has me looking back over my shoulder one more time. A boulder the size of Cincinnati smacks him right in the face, bounces off, and soars like a fucking comet down the mountain.

Barney flings back his head and howls just as my booted heels smack into his soft, orange underbelly. The boulder was enough to daze the fuck out of him, but somehow, he manages to hang on to the side of the cliff. That turns out to be good for me as the leathery skin on his stomach is like a trampoline, just spongy enough to stop my rapid descent and spring me scrabbling back up the hillside.

When I reach the same point where I was when I first fell, I look up to see Duchess sliding down the mountain, her ass resting on one of her foot coverings as she rides it like a hubcap straight toward me. Fuck me, she's an amazing woman. She'd already made it all the way to the top, chunked half the hillside down at Barney, and is now riding in like the cavalry on a piece of space shuttle, screeching to a stop right in front of me.

"My God. You scared me to death, you crazy Scot," she says as she jumps up with the foot covering in her hand. She wraps her arm around my waist and kisses the breath out of me for about four point two seconds before breaking away and attempting to drag me the rest of the way up the mountain.

I'd never admit it, but after skidding half a city block down the rocky hillside on my face, I need the help and lean on her more than I'd really like. But damn, she feels good.

"You saved my life," I tell her as we finally crest the top of the hill.

"You saved mine first," she replies, her head popping back over the edge to smile at me.

I drag myself over and lie there on my back staring at the sky for a minute. I can't believe I'm still alive.

"Well," she says glibly. "That was exciting."

"Somehow, I don't think life with you could ever be boring."

She chuckles. "Believe me, I want it to be. If we ever get out of this, I'm definitely going to try harder."

When I finally stand up, the first thing I notice is the long, broken tree trunk lying half atop a huge dent in the ground.

"That's how I got that last boulder to launch over the side," she explains.

I sigh, not sure whether I should hug her or spank her for putting herself at risk for me again. Of course, if she hadn't, I wouldn't be here to give her a spanking. Though, I'm pretty sure a spanking would make us both feel better.

Barney's howls distract me from sweet thoughts of spankings, and I shuffle over to the ledge and look down.

His size seems to be working against him as he tries everything he can to get to us. Each time he makes some progress, he ends up sliding back down a quarter of the way again. He's pissed now and doesn't mind letting us know about it, either, snarling and snapping and bellowing out threats every time his feet slip.

"Fuck you, Barney! Go find a nice hairy gorocerous or a fat titantula to snack on. Humans are off the menu tonight!"

Duchess smiles and flips him off.

I shake my head, grinning in spite of myself. "Come on, Duchess. Let's go. Or do you want to stand here and taunt Barney the rest of the night."

"Sorry. Bastard tried to eat my man. Can't let that stand."

Her man? I like the sound of that. Chuckling, I wrap my arm around her and limp away into the growing darkness.

Chapter Twenty-two

Epherus

I don't like this. Not one bit. There's a sour taste in my mouth, and a bitter tendril of regret has taken root in my belly and spread throughout me like a disease. Is this what happens when you bond with a human? It must be a side-effect of some kind. I've never felt like this before.

Lisa says it's something called *guilt*? Aurelians certainly do not feel this *guilt*. It's not my fault that the audio wouldn't play after I turned it back on. And I certainly couldn't help it if that conniving bitch Minova took off with Montavi and now, we don't have a clue what they're up to. At least, we can still track them. Sort of.

If this is anyone's fault, it's my amavi's, not mine. How was I supposed to remember to turn the holo-bug back on with her sweet lips wrapped around my cock? If this is any indication of what it will be like having her onboard all the time, I may have to rethink my decision to make her my co-pilot. I can't afford mistakes like this when I'm on a mission. No male alive could keep enough brain cells intact to remember a little detail like turning a spy bot back on when he's got a half-naked Amazon stuck to his dick.

"Okay, stop! We should be right on top of them, according to this thing," she says, tapping her finger on the monitor for emphasis.

I check all the ship's cameras but can't see a damn thing. I even walk around the entire bridge peering out all the windows, and still, nothing.

"I don't understand. We should be able to see them." I stomp back over to my chair and flop down, running my fingers through my hair and growling as I rack my brain. Did I miss a wire or a cable on the docking station? Did I reconnect the UXB line to the right port?

"Your gadget's broken," Lisa states, taking the same path I did as she strolls past all the windows. Her neck cranes forward trying to see the ground directly below us.

"It's not broken," I growl in frustration.

She huffs, spins around, and props her fists on her hips. "Well, what do you call it, then, you big blue lummox? It's not working."

Fuck, she's hot when she's angry. "It's working fine, you sexy little temptress."

She steps toward me slowly, her eyes narrowing as her hand floats toward the stunner at her waist, one that she pilfered from my armory earlier. She doesn't think I know. Her fingers wiggle against the tight-fitting uniform, drawing my eyes to her curvy hips and causing my phila to wriggle with interest.

"Obviously, it's not working fine, or we'd be able to see the ship's lights down there." She points at the floor beneath her feet. "You, you indigo incubus."

I stand up and pace toward her, squinting and smirking. "Okay. You're right. But maybe that's because you fed Minova the radioactive military weapons grade holo-bug prototype instead of dropping it — oh, I don't know — anywhere else in the whole fucking room? You seductive little enchantress."

"All right, that's it," she says, whipping out the stun gun, the barrel charged and lit up as she points it straight at me. "I'm going to have to shoot your spiny ass now, you annoying azure anus."

I laugh. She'd never do that. She wouldn't shoot me. My amavi loves me.

Suddenly, her finger jerks against the trigger, and the stunner whines as it prepares to discharge. Just as I cringe, getting ready to have my ass toasted to a fine blue crisp, the gun fizzles and poots, then dies.

"Well, son-of-a-bitch," she complains, leering at the dark, uncharged barrel before tossing it on the floor and watching it skitter across the room. "Last time I steal a weapon from you."

She cuts her green, hooded eyes back to me, and I can't decide whether to fuck her or spank her. I've never found a female so attractive in my life. Hell, I've never been this hard in my life.

We stand there eyeing each other, my cock pressing so hard against my zipper, I'm afraid it's actually trying to chew a hole through my trousers to get to her. I suppose that means I'm going to fuck her first and spank her later. But first, I need to teach her a lesson. No one can stare down an Aurelian assassin.

Godsdamn! She doesn't even blink. I've had blaster fights with hardened criminals who weren't this dead-eyed and determined. I don't care. I need to establish my dominance with my hot-tempered little amavi. No matter what, I am not going to blink first. Will. Not. Blink.

We attack each other at the same time, dropping to the floor and rolling around like hoghounds in a mud puddle. Fuck! I want to kiss her and lick her all over at once, and for the first time in my life, I wish I had six sets of lips like the Starspongesau race. Or maybe two dicks like the Penisilos. Shit, I'd settle for four sets of hands like the Phalangicans right now.

I tear her shirt over her head with one hard tug, and stuff flies out in all directions. Laserblades, stunners, blasters, even a molecular disbander and some gooey bombs. I didn't even know we had any gooey bombs. I shake it a few more times to make sure all the sensitive weapons are now in a safe pile on the floor in front of me and then fling the shirt somewhere behind me. I stare at the pile of deadly bric-a-brac, unable to believe she could get all of that tucked inside her uniform at one time. Fuck, she turns me on.

I growl and dive back on top of her, attacking her lips, determined to relieve her of the rest of her clothing. My fingers batter at the fastening on her pants, quickly giving up and ripping them off her instead. I shred my shirt as I wrench it over my head and chuck it across the room, her bra whizzing past my ear and landing on top of it.

And then, her glorious, sumptuous breasts lay bare before me, the most beautiful sight I've ever seen. I fall on them like a hungry wolfmonk, nuzzling and nipping, biting and licking. I'm sucking on one nipple and pinching the other when I realize my trousers have somehow disappeared and the little vixen has my cock in her hand, squeezing and pumping and driving me to madness.

"Eff," she moans, and then flips me in the air and slams me flat on my back against the hard metal floor.

We wrestle and grapple for several minutes, rolling around the bridge and taking turns on top of each other until I finally manage to pin her against the navigation console. I hold her hands above her head as my cock slides itself up and down her dripping wet folds.

"Amavi," I groan as my phila wrap around her clit and prod at her sweet little back hole. They vibrate and hum with pleasure.

"Eff," she pants. "Please."

My cock enjoys the sound of our amavi begging and begins to tease at her entrance.

"Please what, little Amazon? Tell me what you want."

She moans as my dick snakes forward, pushing just inside. Just enough to drive us both crazy.

"You," she whispers. "All of you. Inside me. Fuck me, Eff. Fuck me hard."

For once tonight, my amavi and I are in agreement. We groan with ecstasy as I press slowly into her tight, wet channel.

"Don't you dare turn those lights on!" Minova shouts, her voice filling up my bridge and pulling us prematurely from our post-coital cocoon.

Lisa gasps and sits straight up, driving her head into the bottom of the chair that we're lying under. "Ouch! Crap!"

"Shh . . ." I tell her, feeling more than a little grumpy as I reach up to rub the lump on her head. I mean, I'm glad the audio is working again, don't get me wrong. But the last thing I want to hear when I'm lying naked with my amavi after the best sex I've ever had is Minova's whiny bitch voice.

"They hate lights. You'll scare it off. It finally found the path we made, and it has them cornered. The last thing we want is for them to get away again."

"Let's turn it up so we can hear." Montavi's voice comes through loud and clear now, and suddenly, it's joined by the vicious sounds of growling and snarling.

"Is that —"

"A full grown Lacertilia. What are the chances of finding one of those out here? Just listen to it."

"And how often does one get to hear a Lacertilia feed? Especially on live humans." Montavi chuckles.

"What?" Lisa is on her feet now, running around in circles trying to find her clothes.

I clamber to my feet, as well, racing naked over to the camera, dreading what I'm going to see when I get there. I don't know if I'm relieved or more worried when the cameras reveal nothing except darkness.

"Do you see Emily?" Lisa asks, skidding up beside me with a blaster in her hand.

"No. I don't even see Minova's ship," I grouse.

"You have to transport me down there," she tells me as I try resetting the cameras' sensors.

Still, darkness everywhere I look. Could something be blocking the apertures?

"Epherus!"

"What?" I snap, spinning around to look at her.

Sweet Goddess. The sight before me steals my breath away, and my cock doesn't seem to care that we've just finished fucking like a couple of wild raboons. It's ready to go again.

My Amazon stands there with a blaster in each hand, her hair wild and sex-mussed, and her lips all red and swollen from my kisses. Her eyes are practically glowing. She must have given up on finding her own clothes, or they were simply too damaged to wear because my shirt hangs in tattered shreds around her shoulders. Her ample breasts fill it out quite nicely as her nipples peep boldly through the remaining shards of fabric. The shirt ends just above her knees and right above where her black ass-kicking boots pick up.

Godsdamn. She's a mercenary's wet dream.

"Did you hear me?" Her voice is husky and raw from screaming out her passion just moments before. "Get me down there, Eff."

I give my head a shake and force my mind back to the crisis at hand.

"Let me try one more thing."

Crouching beneath the console, I pull out an old thermal infrared imaging sonar that I picked up at a military auction on Aurelia Prime. These devices were once used by off-worlders for long-range surveillance, and though I've never used it before, I'm willing to give just about anything a try right now.

I place it on the console beside the holo-bug dock and connect it to the ship's Marsonium power source. It screeches and groans, but fires up, and immediately shows several green blips on the screen.

"That has to be them," I tell her as I point to the two green dots near the edge of the landscape. "There's Minova's ship, so that has to be Lachlin and Emily."

"Yeah, and there's that fucking tortilla," she says, pointing at the big blip in between them.

"I got it!" I shout, slapping my hands on the table. Spinning around in my chair, I pull out the hand-operated keyboard and type in the override commands for manual control. "I know what to do."

I wrap my fingers tightly around the seldom-used joy stick that emerges from the console in front of me.

"Sit down and buckle up, Amazon. This ride's going to get bumpy."

CHAPTER TWENTY-THREE

Emily

"Stop throwing rocks at it," Lachlin shouts as we race through a thin copse of trees on top of the mountain. "You're only pissing it off more."

"Well, it's better than doing nothing!"

"We are doing something. We're running." He glances behind us and then grabs my arm, sprinting forward with a renewed burst of speed and pulling me along with him.

"How the hell did it get up here in the first place?"

He shakes his head. "I don't know for sure, but if I had to guess, I'd say up the side of the mountain they melted."

This is insane. We got away. We were being rescued. At least, we thought we were. Barney was stuck at the bottom of the ravine, and a rescue ship arrived on the scene. Except the rescue ship didn't rescue us.

It appeared out of nowhere, blasting away with its laser cannons. We thought it was shooting at Barney, but turns out they were just firing into the side of the mountain. We thought they were here to save us, but now, they've turned off their lights and are just hovering there watching us. Do they not realize this dragonasaur is about to eat us?

"There's the cave," Lachlin shouts, pointing at a hole in a rock wall several yards in front of us. "We could try to hide."

"Or, get trapped inside," I groan.

"We could try our luck out here, too," he agrees. "There might be a trail down the mountain on the other side of those rocks. Come on. Keep up," he tells me as we weave our way through the trees.

Keep up, my ass. I only let him lead so I can watch his butt jiggle while we run. That's the only reason. Still, I let him keep point, and we continue on that way for a while, making pretty decent progress. By the time we reach the other side, Barney has disappeared, and I feel like we can finally breathe again. Oh, I'm sure he's still around, but he's not on our tails anymore. Thank goodness, too, because we come out of the trees into a freaking rock garden, several of them taller than me.

"It's like this mountain hates us," I grumble.

"Here." He puts his hand up my dress and pushes my large booty over the top of one of the boulders. "Keep going."

We keep on like this for at least a quarter of a mile until I either have to sit down and rest or burrow beneath one of these rocks and hide. I stop running and bend over to pant while I pinch my side. It's full-on nighttime now, no light except for the stars and moons above us. Maybe we'll get lucky and Barney won't be able to see well in the dark.

"Duchess," Lachlin says. "We need to keep going."

"You go ahead without me. I'll catch up," I tell him. Though, I wouldn't have said it if I thought for a second he actually would.

He looks around nervously and nods. "Okay. Let's rest. Just for a minute."

"Just for a minute," I agree, highly doubting I'll ever move again as long as I live, which may turn out to be not very long at all.

I stare up at the ship that's still just sitting there, hovering above us. I don't understand why they don't do something, either transport us up, transport themselves down, shoot Barney, send us some weapons, something, *anything*.

"What the hell are they doing up there?"

Lachlin shakes his head. "I don't know. It's Horok's ship,

though. Or, at least, one of his fleet."

"Maybe it's malfunctioning, and they can't get to us?"

He shakes his head, hesitant to say what I already know. The ship is working fine.

"I just can't figure out why they aren't helping us."

"I don't know. Other than not having any lights, it doesn't appear to have anything wrong with it."

"But they had lights on earlier, didn't they?"

"Yeah." He frowns at the ship and nods. "It doesn't make any sense."

"Here's what I know," I grouse. "If Cora and Lisa are up there, I'm going to kick their asses all the way back to the castle when I get my hands on them."

"I'll help you." He chuckles.

We stare at the ship for a minute longer, and then, Lachlin says the words I've been dreading.

"We need to keep moving."

I sigh and nod. "I know. I'm just so tired of all this, I could—"

"Shit!" Lachlin shouts as Godzillasaurus leaps over a giant boulder and lands about twenty yards in front of us.

He grabs my hand and shoots off like a bullet, me in tow. I forget about my tired body, my aching feet, and my abused lungs. All I can think about now is the whiplash I just endured when he jerked me so hard, I flew twenty yards before my feet ever hit the ground.

One thing we discover quickly, Barney may not be a good mountain climber, but he can certainly navigate the smaller rocks very well. What he doesn't stomp on, he jumps over. So by the time we make it to the end of the rock yard, there's nowhere left to run.

We've reached the other side of the mountain, which could actually be the edge of Tarilax, from the looks of it. It's not nearly as human-friendly as the other side, and Barney is right behind us.

"Uh . . . should we take a chance and jump?" I glance over my shoulder. Nothing but a sheer drop-off behind us and only darkness below.

"Death by lizard, or death by skull fracture? I'm not sure I like either of those choices."

Barney roars, and I swear the son-of-a-bitch is laughing as he creeps closer to us. Lachlin grabs my arms and pulls me to him, his face right in mine.

"Listen to me. When I tell you, I want you to run. As fast you can, just run. Do you hear me?" He gives me a shake.

What the hell is he saying? I wag my head. "No fucking way. I'm not leaving you."

"Dammit, Duchess." He looks like he might kill me himself for a moment, then he leans in and kisses me, hard and fast. "I love you, Emily. I'm sorry I let you down."

I give him a crumbly smile and shake my head. "You never let me down, Lachlin."

Barney finally tires of playing with his food and moves in for the final kill. I keep my eyes on Lachlin. If his face is the last thing I see when I leave this world, well, I could do a lot worse.

Suddenly, his features are bathed in a soft, glowing light that begins to slowly spill out around us. Glorious light from down in the valley behind us, light so bright it spreads out several feet in front of us. I gasp and turn toward Barney, who's cringing back away from the ledge, away from us, and back into the shadows.

"Oh my gosh." I laugh. "He doesn't like the light."

"Un-fucking-believable," Lachlin yips.

"What is that?"

"That's Tartopia," he says, peering over the side of the cliff at the valley. "Tonight's the Festival of Lights. I totally forgot about it."

"Well, it's official. That's my favorite Tarilean holiday from now on."

Barney slinks further back away from the lights, tossing his head and snarling, but not completely giving up. He paces back and forth just on the other side of the shadows, waiting to see if it gets dark again, I'm sure. I totally understand — he's worked way too hard for this meal to just walk away. But I've decided I don't want to be Barney food tonight.

"Okay, what do we do now?"

"See that opening in the rocks over there?" He points to a gap not more than ten or fifteen yards away, and I nod.

"Let's make — "

Suddenly, the hovering ship above us fires off a single shot and then begins to move. I think for one joyous moment that it's finally going to save us. It's finally going to pick us up and get us the hell out of here. But then, it stops right between us and the valley behind us and slowly adjusts its position until it's fully absorbing the light from the valley below. Then, we're cast into darkness once again, and the shadows in front of us begin to move. Barney has found his opening.

Gasping, I turn around and wave my hands at them. "No. Move! You're blocking the light!"

"Fuck," Lachlin grumbles as he grabs my arm and pushes me toward the rock pathway. "Run, Duchess!"

We take off sprinting toward the opening, but the ship follows, slowly pacing us as we run, giving Barney ample time to cut us off. And he doesn't waste the opportunity.

"Godsdammit," Lachlin shouts as we pull up short once again.

I watch as he looks around in desperation, and my hopes are dashed again. I can't do this anymore. We can't catch a break. I give up.

"I'm sorry, Duchess. I don't know who they are, but they've royally fucked us again."

Just as Barney positions himself at the edge, stretching his long neck toward Lachlin, a blinding bright light creeps over the edge of the mountain behind him. Like a midnight sun, it crawls higher into the sky until the entire mountaintop is flooded with light.

"Look! It's another ship!" Lachlin points at the sky above the hovering vessel, which is also now lit up. "It's Eff!"

Barney howls and stumbles around blindly along the edge of the cliff until the soft ground gives way beneath him. His angry roar is the last we hear as he tumbles over the side into the darkness below.

"Eff!" I laugh and cry at the same time, hugging Lachlin with one hand and waving at the ship like a fool with the other as I thank my lucky stars for friends like Eff.

When the hovering craft begins to whine, we look up to a laser-cannon appearing from a small window beneath the hull. The sound of the whirring cannon echoes across the mountaintop as the laser site locks on to its target — locks on to me and Lachlin.

"Godsdammit," Lachlin huffs, and we take off running once again.

CHAPTER TWENTY-FOUR

Lisa

"Fuck!" Eff shouts after the ship stops rocking. "They just took out the transporter."

"Now they're firing at Emily and Lachlin!" I scream as several large boulders explode on the ground below. "Shoot them, Eff! Take them out!"

"I can't," he shouts back. "I can't open fire on a royal spacecraft. They'll lock us up and throw away the key."

"I don't care. At least, our friends will be alive!"

"Which is more than we'll be after the Aurelian government gets ahold of us and tries us for treason once we set off an intergalactic war."

Okay, I've had it. I'm tired of tortillas trying to eat my friends and bitches plotting to kill us for breathing. I'm sick of this planet and everything on it that has teeth longer than two inches, present company excluded. If we can't even protect ourselves when we're being shot at, I'll take matters into my own hands.

"Get me down there," I tell him using every commanding, authoritative muscle I have in my vocal chords.

"On the ground? Are you crazy? What can you do from there except get shot at?"

I shake my head. "Not on the ground, Eff. On their ship. Get me on their ship."

"Are you nut—"

An explosion on the ground rocks the bridge, and I stumble

169

forward, bracing myself on his chair.

"Get me down there, or I swear, Eff, I'll never speak to you again."

He eyes me uncertainly, I'm sure judging whether or not I'm bluffing. I'm not, and the long sigh he gives lets me know that he's come to the correct conclusion.

"I'll go," he says. "You stay here, and I'll go."

I shake my head. "I can't pilot the ship."

"All you have to do is keep it in the air," he says. "I'll show you how."

"No way. Not unless you want to see me crash in a fiery ball against their ship or into the side of this mountain."

"Fuck!" He frowns for a moment and then growls as he pulls open a drawer in the console and scours through a bunch of junk inside.

"I got this," I assure him. "Just get me close to their ship, Eff. I'll take it from there."

"Here, wear this," he says, reaching for a small holo-cam and pinning it to my shirt. "Put this piece in your ear. I won't be able to hear you, but you'll be able to hear me. At least I can see what you're seeing with the holo-cam and talk you through the logistics."

I give him a nod and take the earpiece. "You're doing the right thing."

He shakes his head. "Maybe you're right. Maybe we should just shoot them down and haul ass to the next galaxy."

"No. We're not running. I can do this, baby. Trust me. It's what I do." I lean in and kiss his lips before stepping toward the exit.

"Go to the loading bay and open the escape hatch, Amazon. Wait there until I flash the lights."

"Got it," I shout over my shoulder as I walk out of the bridge and head for the loading bay.

I do a systematic weapons check along the way. I've

already inspected each one of them, took them apart and re-assembled them, making sure they were charged and working properly. I walk through the empty ship patting every pocket and secret compartment and grabbing extra supplies from the armory as I pass.

By the time I get to the loading bay and wrench open the hatch, I'm shaking with excitement. I love it. I've always been a bit of a sensation seeker. I get high off the danger, intoxicated by the fear, and thrilled by the rush of adrenaline. It's the only time I feel totally alive. Well, it used to be the only time. Eff is now my drug of choice.

"Get your head in the game, Lisa!" I give my head a little shake. The only thing that should be on my mind right now is getting my hands on that wicked bitch, Minova, and her evil minions.

I look down just as said wicked bitch's ship appears in the open hatch. We crawl to a stop and sit there hovering for a minute. My body twitches, my skin itches, and I'm not sure I can wait much longer. Finally, the loading bay lights flash off and on, and I smile. That's my cue.

I wriggle my body through the opening and hang there for a moment while I give myself another short pep talk. Then, I let go, drop onto the top of Minova's ship, and flatten myself against the external hull. The wind is blowing so hard, I'm not sure whether I can stand up without blowing off.

I belly-crawl over to the side and place a welder's tab in between two small grooves. I remove the pin from the tab and snap the seal. Immediately, it blazes to life, expanding right before my eyes, and melting a hole in the ship big enough for me to squeeze through. I have to hurry now. No doubt the breach will set off the alarms.

By the time my boots hit the floor, I already have a gooey bomb in one hand and a stunner in the other. I first reached for the molecular disbander, but then remembered what Eff said about causing an international incident. So I put it back like a good girl. I'll have to try and do this without killing anyone.

"Don't move," a deep, masculine voice snarls from behind me.

Without hesitating, I spin around and punch him right in the throat with my stunner. Then, I shoot his stupid ass with it. Fortunately, the stunner works this time, and Guard Number One is out of commission for a while.

Looking around the room, I figure I've landed in someone's quarters. A guard's room, from the looks of it. Unmade bunk bed, wrinkled clothes all over the floor, dirty dishes on the bedside table, it reminds me of home. I step over the snoozing guard and make it all the way to the door before I hear a small army of boots stomping toward me. Fuck, I don't have time for this.

I pull out the little flap from the gooey bomb and pinch the nipple on the end. Then, I reach my arm around the doorway and toss it in the direction of the guards. The bomb skips down the hall like a flat rock on water just as several of them shout out a warning. There's no time to react before it explodes. I step out from the doorway firing my stunner, just in case anyone made it through clean. No one did, though. Two of them are pinned to the floor, and the other two are glued to the walls, the surprised expressions on their faces telling me they clearly didn't expect that.

"Good job, baby."

I jump and nearly scream, forgetting about Eff in my ear. Shit, that would not have been cool.

"Look alive, Amazon. There are two guards heading your way," Eff says. "Go left down the next hall and then right at the end of that one."

Oh, I like this. I take off like a streak, beating it down the hallway as instructed. When I get to the end, I wait there for him to tell me my next move.

"Okay, now you're going to have to go into that shaft there on your right. There should be a hatch or a vent or something. See it?"

Sure enough, on my right, there's a small airshaft with a vented cover over it. "Yeah, I see it."

I fumble around for a moment, looking for a latch. There's not one. It's sealed up tighter than a young virgin's thighs. My patience waning, I haul back my boot and kick the shit out of it. It makes a dent, but obviously isn't going to be muscled out of the way that easily. I grab my last welder's tab and slap it onto one of the slats, praying it will work since the surface isn't solid.

"That's not going to work," Eff says in my ear. "There's too much space in between the slats."

He's right. The tab only melts away two slats, not nearly enough for me to get inside. Fuck it. I pull out my blaster and shoot the damn thing, then I kick it until it comes loose. It crashes to the floor with a clang loud enough to wake up the dead.

"Watch out! Two guards coming in fast on your six."

I spin around just in time to catch a fist to the edge of my chin. It connects well enough to send me reeling backwards, though. I trip on the vent cover and go down.

Apparently, they're done fucking around, too. When he raises his blaster, I have no choice but to shoot. It's either him or me. The other one makes a dive at me, his elbow up and ready to crush my larynx. I manage to roll out of the way just in time for him to hit the floor instead, but that doesn't stop him from grabbing a fistful of my hair and trying to pound the blaster out of my hand.

"Really? My hair?" I snipe. "What are you? A little bitch?"

He finally wrenches the blaster from my hand after he wraps the other one around my neck and starts squeezing. I sacrifice it gladly for the laserblade in my shirt pocket, slapping it open quickly before I pass out. The cocky bastard thinks I'm done for and gives my head one final shake, knocking my head against the floor, before he stands up on his knees beside me.

He raises the blaster and points it at my head, a gruesome smile on his face. "You fucked up, little human."

No fucking way are they taking me out like this. "Yeah, I know. I should've brought some percussion bombs."

I fling my arm around, and the laserblade hums as it slices through the guard's wrist. He squeals like a pig, a surprised pig, grasping at his arm and trying to stand. I lift my leg and boot him right in the chest, sending him sprawling into the wall across the hallway. Then, I pick up my blaster, his hand still attached to it, aim, and squeeze the trigger. More like squeeze his finger since it's still attached to the trigger. But whatever. There's one more down.

"There's two more guards heading your way. Go, Amazon. Into the shaft. Quick."

I dive into the shaft, which is just big enough for me to run through it hunched over like an old crone. It's damp and musty, and the floor is slick. It's also pitch black inside. If it weren't for the light on my blaster, I'd be running blind. The shaft goes straight for about twenty feet and then branches off in two directions. I stop when I come to the fork, waiting for Eff to tell me which way to go.

"Eff! Which way?"

I know he can't hear me, but he isn't saying anything. I'm about to make a guess and go left when I hear him pant into my ear, "Left! Go left!"

Suddenly, the ship rattles and shakes as if we've been hit by massive gunfire. What the fuck was that?

"Sorry, Amavi. She had them pinned. I had to shoot."

Sorry, he says. Like I'd be mad about that? The shaft ends

about thirty or so feet from the last turn, another slatted cover blocking off the exit.

"Behind you, Amazon. Look out!"

I can't exactly spin around. Hell, I can barely move at all. I pull a gooey bomb out from between my tits, give it a little kiss, then chuck it between my legs. I hear it bounce one time behind me before the sound of blaster fire fills the shaft.

The gooey bomb explodes at the same time as the pain in my shoulder, slamming me into the vent cover. The cover gives, and I fall flat on my face into another hallway, screaming out in agony.

"Amazon! Amavi!" I hear Eff shouting in my earpiece.

"Eff," I moan.

"Lisa! Are you all right? Can you get up? Lisa!"

CHAPTER TWENTY-FIVE

Epherus

Shit! That dirty son-of-a-claffer! I was too caught up trying to keep an eye on Lachlin and Emily and making sure Minova didn't leave the bridge. I didn't even see the other two guards coming up behind her until it was too late.

"Please, Amazon. Please, get up."

She's not moving, and from where she's lying, all I can see is a growing pool of blood spreading out slowly across the floor in front of her.

My hearts are turning to stone in my chest, ice filling up my veins. I can't breathe very well now. I need to get to my amavi. I can't live without her. I don't want to live without her. There's something tickling my cheek. I reach up to wipe my hand across my face, and my fingers come away with liquid on them. What the fuck?

My eyes are leaking. Is this part of human bonding, too? I stare at them for a moment, glad for them. I don't even care. I just want my amavi to get up, to be okay. I'll kill every fucker onboard that ship if she doesn't get through this. I'll kill Minova, and then, I'll track down Irston, Irston's mother, his father, every family member, every dirty Council member on Tarilax until—"

Gasping, I grab the monitor with both hands. I see the floor, her knees, and then the other end of the hallway. She's up! Thank the goddess. My amavi is alive. She's all right.

"Amazon!" My voice sounds strained and hoarse. A huge

lump has settled in my throat, and it's extremely difficult to talk around. "You have to get out of there, my love. Go. Now!"

I watch as she leans against the wall for a moment, bending over with her hands propped against her thighs. I curse the cameras for not allowing me to see her or her wounds. I need to see her.

"Come on, baby. You can do this. You're almost there."

She stands up straight, reaches out one more time to steady herself against the wall, and then starts walking crooked toward the end of the hall.

"That's it. That's the bridge just ahead," I tell her. "It's too sturdy to kick in, and I'm not sure your blaster is strong enough to get through it."

The view on the monitor is shaky, like she's having trouble staying up. Fuck, I need to get down there. Could the autopilot hold us here long enough for me to go and get her? I don't have time to decide before she reaches the door.

"There's two of them inside, Amazon, and two more coming down the airshaft behind you. You're in no shape to fight all of them. Just get some place and hide. I'm coming for you."

That must not have set well with her. The stubborn creature spins around again and starts stumbling back toward the airshaft. She stops a few feet away and drops to her knees. For a horrible second, I think she's passing out again, but then, her arms extend, her hands wrapped around the stunner. Then, one of the guards steps out of the shaft.

I see the little red dot settle right between his eyes, and he drops like a bag of rocks. The other one must be firing at her. I can't hear it, but the wall beside her explodes into flames, and she starts to roll across the floor. Is she hit? What the fuck are those blasters charged with? Finally, I see the bastard. He bursts from the shaft, blaster in his hand as he turns to face us. Laser trails light up the hall, and I clench the monitor so hard, the frame begins to crack.

"No!"

Suddenly, he freezes, the blaster falls out of his grip, and he slips to his knees. That's when I notice the hilt of the laser-blade sticking out from his chest. He falls over onto his side, and Amazon starts shuffling toward him. She leans down, pulls out her laserblade, and wipes it against his shirt before flicking it shut and stuffing it back into her pocket. Then, she bends down again and picks up the dead guard's blaster. She weighs it in her hand for a moment and turns around and heads back toward the bridge.

"Good job, sweetheart. Now, try a welder's tab on the door," I tell her.

I expect her to stop, pull out another welder's tab, and stick it to the door, but she doesn't. Instead, she raises the blaster she took from the guard and fires it at the door as she strolls casually toward it. It explodes into a shower of splintered fragments, and Amazon dives inside. We must roll for several feet, the camera just a blur of body parts and carpet and flashes of ceiling until she springs to her feet and I see her fling something toward the center of the room. A gooey bomb.

It hits a support beam right beside Montavi's head and ex-plodes, encasing him in a spidery green web. I sigh with relief until I see that somehow Montavi's hand is clear and there's a blaster in it. His finger twitches against the trigger, firing off laser blasts in every direction. Minova spins around, blaster in her hand, shouting something as she fires at Montavi. His head explodes like an overripe tomadish, and the wild laser fire ceases.

While Minova stares at Montavi, Amazon jumps onto a console and leaps through the air, crashing into her and nail-ing her to the floor before she has a chance to fire off another shot. They roll around on the ground wrestling over the blaster for what seems like forever. Once again, I curse the damn camera when I can't see anything but a flurry of clothes and skin.

Finally, Amazon straddles Minova, punches her in the face, and wrests the blaster from her grip. I watch it fly across the room and explode into pieces when Amazon flings it at the wall. Then, her fist flies through the air, landing in Minova's face over and over and over. I let her have as much satisfaction as I can before I'm forced to intervene.

"Amavi, stop," I tell her to no avail. "Amazon! Stop! You'll kill her."

Finally, she stops and stands up slowly, raking her arm across her mouth as she stares down at Minova. Then, she gives her one last kick in the ribs before making her way over to the central coms station. My coms unit screeches once, and my Amazon's voice fills the bridge.

"Eff, get down there and pick them up," she commands as her holographic image appears in front of me. "Then you can talk me through how to land this stupid thing."

"Okay. Are you all right, my love?"

She nods, smiling. "Yeah, I think I'll live. I haven't decided yet if she will, though."

I can see the entire bridge now in the holo-image. Minova's unconscious body lies prostrate on the floor next to Montavi's headless one. My amavi's shirt is burnt and bloody where a laser blast caught her in the shoulder. It looks bad, but she's mobile and able to lift her arm, so I think she'll be all right until I can get her into Medical.

"I'm not sure how we're going to explain this," I tell her honestly. "But we'll figure it out."

"Are there any more guards left over here?"

"No. Montavi was the last one. Go secure the survivors and meet me back here in ten. I'm landing now."

She nods. "Okay, and Eff?"

"Yes, my love?"

"Thank you."

"This was all you, my sexy little assassin." And she is, too. I've never seen a more beautiful sight in my life. I can't wait to get her back here where we can be alone and take our time.

"Pfft. You're a strange man, Epherus Zinto."

"I'm not a man," I tell her. "I'm an Aurelian, and if you don't know the difference by now, I'll have to remind you when I get you back onboard."

She giggles, blood dripping down her arm and a blaster in each hand. She's so fucking cute, I can't stand it.

"See you in ten," she says as she reaches out to term the com.

Gods, I love that female. I'm smiling and humming as I enter the coordinates for the landing gear. I set down a few seconds later and open the external hatch, whistling as I leave the bridge to go find our long-lost friends. It doesn't take long. In fact, I don't even get down the gangway before Emily pounces on me.

"Eff! Oh my God!" She throws her arms around my neck and squeezes so hard, I think she may be trying to dislodge my head from the rest of my body. "I've never been so happy to see anyone in my life!"

"Okay, then," I grumble, patting her lightly on the back. "That's enough."

I try to peel her off me, but she's stuck like tsatsa fly paper. I don't care much for these public displays of affection, and besides, I'm a mated male. I should never be locked in the arms of any female except my amavi. I scowl over her shoulder at Lachlin, who's smiling from ear to ear as he walks onto the boarding plank with us.

"Eff! Man, it's so good to see you!"

"I am not a man," I remind him again with a sigh. "Now, kindly remove your female from my neck so we can get out of here."

"Are you by yourself?" Emily asks as she finally releases me.

"Lisa is aboard the other vessel," I tell them as we reenter the ship.

"Lisa?" Lachlin asks with surprise.

"Why the hell didn't she help us, then?" Emily asks, suddenly vexed.

I scowl at the simpering female. "What do you mean? She saved you."

"She did nothing," Lachlin argues. "She blasted a path for that fucking T-Rex to waltz right up the mountain side and then sat there hovering and watching while the damn thing tried to eat us."

"That wasn't Lisa," I growl, trying to restrain myself. "That was Minova."

"Minova?" they say at the same time as we step onto the bridge.

"Yes, Minova," I reply, flipping on the coms and smiling as my amavi's image appears before us.

"Emily!" she shouts, and the other female shrieks and jumps up and down. "Lachlin! You guys scared us to death."

"Lisa! Oh my God. You're hurt!" Emily says.

I listen to them shriek at each other for a while, then I turn to Lachlin. He looks like hell, his clothes torn and bloody, and he has bruises, cuts and scrapes covering most of his exposed skin. He obviously needs at least a full day in the Rejuvenator 3000.

"You are all right, Lachlin MacTavish?"

He nods and smiles. "I'll live. I'm just worried about my mate."

"Your mate?" I cut my eyes to Emily who's still chattering away at Amazon. I suppose I could see this female with my friend, as long as she makes him happy. My amavi definitely thinks highly of her, so there must be something good about her. "I see. You believe she is the one, then? Your fated mate?"

"I know she is. She's a gift from the goddess."

I nod, smiling in spite of myself as I pat him on the shoulder. "Then you're lucky indeed, and I'm glad to hear it. Now, I need you and your mate to help me get my mate back over here on this ship where she belongs."

"Your mate?" He cuts his eyes to Lisa's holo-image.

I nod again, smirking at my good fortune. "Yes. You're not the only one who was smiled upon by a goddess."

"The goddess of fertility? Urgowa?"

"No, Sheirlah. The goddess of war."

EPILOGUE

Emily

Dang! These hospital chairs are about as comfortable as a cold hard slab of concrete. I groan and shift around, fanning myself with a piece paper until Lachlin finally turns to look at me.

"You okay, babe?"

"Yeah, I guess. Sorry. It's just hard to sit in one place like this for so long."

"Tell me about it." Lisa nods in agreement, shifting her belly toward me and her back toward Eff.

It's hard to believe we're both only four months along. Well, it's hard to believe Lisa is only four months. I barely have a good baby bump. She looks more like she's eight months, which has something to do with Aurelian births usually taking only six.

"Do it, blue guy," she says to him over her shoulder.

I giggle as I watch Eff turn sideways in his chair and start rubbing her back. I need to train Lachlin to do that.

"Do you want to sit in my lap?" This is Lachlin's answer to every pregnancy malady I have these days.

"No, thank you. If my memory serves me correctly, that's what got us into this mess in the first place."

Lachlin chuckles. "Hang in there, Duchess. With any hope, it won't be too much longer."

"I can't believe it's taking this long. It's not like it's her first one," Aine says as she paces in front of us with baby Theo.

"I'm not sure Tarilean babies adhere to a definite timetable," Griz says thoughtfully.

"Give me that boy," Bruce tells Aine, giving Li'Andra a pat on the leg as he stands. "He wants to play with his Papa and his Yaya."

"Look! There's Maggie!" Shauna leaps from her chair and runs toward the double doors of the delivery room, as if Lisa or I might actually try to race her there.

I look at Lisa and frown. "Seriously?"

"Eff, get up and help me up," Lisa whines.

I watch, fascinated, as he does it without any hesitation. These are great tips for me to employ here in a few months.

Lachlin laughs and shakes his head. "Don't be getting any ideas."

It's really scary how that man can read my mind sometimes.

"Oh, I have ideas," I tell him. "You'll do them and be glad for the opportunity."

"Hey guys!" Maggie steps through the doors looking like a supermodel. No one would ever guess she's been back there for the past three hours delivering Cora's fourth baby.

"What is it? More triplets? Twins? Boy? Girl?" Shauna fires off a list of questions before Maggie can even remove her coat.

"All I can tell you is that it's healthy and it looks like Horok," she informs us. "He's going to be here in a minute to give you all the details."

"How's Cora?" I ask.

"She's fine. Just tired. This one was quite a bit bigger than the other three."

"Okay, you said *it* and *one*?" Shauna jumps on the clues like Detective Sherlock. "So, is it a boy or a girl?"

Maggie rolls her eyes just as Horok walks through the door wearing a set of scrubs with two tiny footprints inked above a pink sticker announcing we have a girl.

"It's a girl!" we all cry at the same time, trying to wedge in around him to hear the details.

"We have a new princess in the royal family," he says proudly. "Thirteen stones and twenty-two enbars long. She is healthy, and her name is India."

"India?" Lisa screws up her face, and I elbow her in the arm.

"We said we weren't going to make fun of names," I remind her.

"Princess India," Shauna says. "I like it. It's pretty. When can we see her?"

"They're cleaning her up now. Give them a few minutes, and you can go back. She is very beautiful, except . . ."

"Except what?" Lisa asks incredulously.

He better be careful. India has four over-protective aunts standing here that won't hesitate to take him down.

"She looks like my father." Horok chuckles.

"Speaking of, where is your father?" Bruce asks.

"He is helping deal with Irston's latest Motion for Dismissal," Horok explains as he gives me and Lachlin an apologetic smile. "I am truly sorry I wasn't able to keep Minova in prison. But I do intend to make sure it's where she ends up."

"Don't worry about it," Lisa says. "You have about six months to take care of Minova before we're in any shape to take action on our own."

"Yeah, and it will take me at least that long to reconstruct the serum," Shauna says. "And that's with Maggie's help, whenever she isn't busy delivering babies."

"There will be no taking action on your own," Horok scolds. "Our younglings need their dam at home, and I need my amavi."

"Yeah, yeah. Fine," Lisa waves him off. "We'll take care of your amavi."

"That's good because I need you to stay with her tonight

while I go meet with the Aurelian premier," he says. "I won't be long. Cora and India should rest until I get back."

"Sure." Lisa smiles, and the rest of us nod our agreement.

Horok cuts his eyes to Eff. "And I would like for you to accompany me, too, Epherus."

I look at Eff who is scowling, as usual. He gives Horok a quick nod.

"Of course," he says. "Has Prince Oaryundu admitted to his part in the scheme?"

"Not as such, but I believe King Perigresh knows it to be true. He's offered to help fund efforts to reconstruct the original formula, as well as generous resources such as scientists, laboratory equipment and tools. They're basically opening their doors to Shauna and Maggie. They want to partner with Tarilax to get the vaccine to everyone who needs it, everywhere. If we can pull this off, Epherus, it would be the first joint venture between our two planets in the entire histories of our people."

Lisa grabs Eff's hand, smiling brightly as she squeezes his arm. "And you'll be part of it, Eff. Honey, that's wonderful."

I think I almost see him smile.

"Hey! Are you guys coming in or not?" Aine pokes her head out from the double doors and smiles at us.

"Oh! Be right there!" I shout before turning to Lachlin. "Are you coming in with us?"

"Wouldn't miss it." He chuckles. "I've got to see this baby that looks like King Jorga."

We don't take two steps before said king storms around the corner with a long line of guards trailing behind him. And unless I'm totally misreading the worried look on his face, this isn't a social call.

"Horok!"

"Sire. What's wrong?"

King Jorga orders his men to stand down as he approaches

our group. As comfortable as I am around Horok, King Jorga is a different story. At barbecues and dinner parties, when he's playing grandpa to all the kids, is one thing. But like this? When he's being all kingy? Well, I nestle into Lachlin, squeezing myself beneath his arm where I feel safe.

"We've got trouble," King Jorga tells Horok. "There's an Iwoehan fleet blocking the trade route through Warlsafh."

"But that's the primary thoroughfare to Aurelia," Horok replies.

King Jorga nods. "And we're already missing several ships. I checked with Perigresh and the Aurelians are, too. We've just received confirmation from an Iwoehan vessel called the Dracarus that they've confiscated the crews and the cargos, but they say they are willing to negotiate the terms of a prisoner exchange."

"Prisoner exchange?" Horok growls. "We don't have any high-profile prisoners. Who would dare risk an intergalactic war for a meager prisoner exchange?"

My heart drops as Lachlin and Epherus stare silently at each other. Then, they both speak at the same time.

"Aliyah."

ABOUT THE AUTHOR

Wife, mother, and avid animal lover, D. Morrissey was born and raised in small-town Arkansas, just a stone's throw away from Little Rock. A business executive by day, she spends most of her nights penning steamy romance novels. While her books cover various genres from contemporary mystery to sci-fi fantasy, you will find the prevailing themes through all include smart, funny females and hot, loyal males. Her list of credits includes Rhone, His Goddess, His Warrior Princess, His Sexy Duchess, Insanity Plea, Just Plain Crazy, All That Sparkles, Liar, and Deceiver.